PEN

Mozart's

Eduard Mörike (1804–75) was the seventh child of a large family in Ludwigsburg (Württemberg). His father was a doctor who died when Mörike was thirteen. He studied theology in Tübingen and became a Protestant pastor in 1834, a profession in which he was seldom happy and from which he retired after nine years. His novel *Maler Noten* was published in 1832 and a first volume of poetry in 1838. Between 1851 and 1866 he taught literature at a seminary in Stuttgart, and continued to write, including his masterpiece *Mozart's Journey to Prague* (1855). Mörike never travelled beyond his native Württemberg and led a quiet and increasingly reclusive life with his Catholic wife and two daughters. He spent the last decade of his life in virtual solitude, anxious to avoid the fame his writing had brought him.

EDUARD MÖRIKE

Mozart's Journey
to Prague

Translated by David Luke

PENGUIN BOOKS

PENGUIN BOOKS

Published by the Penguin Group
Penguin Books Ltd, 80 Strand, London WC2R ORL, England
Penguin Group (USA) Inc., 375 Hudson Street, New York, New York 10014, USA
Penguin Group (Canada), 90 Eglinton Avenue East, Suite 700,
Toronto, Ontario, Canada M4P 2Y3 (a division of Pearson Penguin Canada Inc.)
Penguin Ireland, 25 St Stephen's Green, Dublin 2, Ireland
(a division of Penguin Books Ltd)
Penguin Group (Australia), 250 Camberwell Road, Camberwell, Victoria 3124,
Australia (a division of Pearson Australia Group Pty Ltd)
Penguin Books India Pvt Ltd, 11 Community Centre,
Panchsheel Park, New Delhi – 110 017, India
Penguin Group (NZ), cnr Airborne and Rosedale Roads, Albany,
Auckland 1310, New Zealand (a division of Pearson New Zealand Ltd)
Penguin Books (South Africa) (Pty) Ltd, 24 Sturdee Avenue,
Rosebank, Johannesburg 2196, South Africa

Penguin Books Ltd, Registered Offices: 80 Strand, London WC2R ORL, England

www.penguin.com

First published by Libris 1997
Revised edition published by Penguin Books 2003
Published as a Penguin Red Classic 2006

1

Translation copyright © David Luke, 1997, 2003
All rights reserved

The moral right of the translator has been asserted

Set in MT Dante
Typeset by Palimpsest Book Production Limited, Polmont, Stirlingshire
Printed in England by Clays Ltd, St Ives plc

ISBN 13: 978–0–14102–348–9
ISBN 10: 0–14102–348–1

In the autumn of 1787 Mozart, accompanied by his wife, travelled to Prague, where he was to stage the first production of *Don Giovanni*.

On the third day of their journey, at about eleven o'clock in the morning of 14 September and not more than thirty hours distant from Vienna, the couple were driving in the best of spirits in a north-westerly direction, beyond the Mannhardsberg and the German Thaya, not far from Schrems and the highest point of the beautiful Moravian mountains.

'Their carriage,' writes Baroness von T— to her friend, 'a handsome orange-yellow vehicle drawn by three post-horses, was the property of a certain old lady, the wife of General Volkstett, who always seems to have rather prided herself on her acquaintance with the Mozart family and the favours she has shown to them.' This imprecise description of the conveyance in question is one to which a connoisseur of the taste of the 1780s may well be able to add a few details. The doors on both sides of the yellow coach were decorated with floral bouquets painted in their natural colours, and it was edged with narrow gold trimming, but the paintwork in general was still quite without that glossy lacquered finish favoured by modern Viennese carriage-builders. The body moreover was not fully rounded out, though lower down it curved inwards with coquettish boldness; the roof was high and the windows had rigid leather curtains, though at present these were drawn back.

Here we might also make some mention of the costumes of the two travellers. Frau Constanze, carefully saving her husband's new clothes for special occasions, had packed these in the trunk and chosen a modest outfit for him to wear: over an embroidered waistcoat of rather faded blue his usual brown topcoat with its row of large buttons, each fashioned in a starlike pattern with a layer of red-gold pinchbeck glinting through the outer material; black silk breeches and stockings, and shoes with gilt buckles. The weather being quite unusually hot for the time of year, he had removed his coat and for the last half hour had been sitting bareheaded and in shirt sleeves, chattering content-edly. Madame Mozart was wearing a comfortable travelling dress, light green with white stripes. Loosely bound, her beautiful auburn hair fell in abundant curls over her neck and shoulders; all her life she had never disfigured it with powder, but her husband's vigorous growth of hair, tied in a pigtail, was today merely powdered more casually than usual.

The road rose gently between the fertile fields which here and there intersected the wooded land-scape; at a leisurely pace they had reached the top and were now at the forest's edge.

'I wonder,' said Mozart, 'how many woods we've passed through, today and yesterday and the day before yesterday! I've never given them a thought, still less did it occur to me to get out and set foot in them. But now, my darling, let's do just that, and pick some of those bluebells growing so prettily in the shade. Coachman! Give your horses a bit of a rest!'

As they both stood up, a minor disaster came to light for which the maestro was soundly scolded. By his carelessness, a phial of very expensive eau-de-Cologne had lost its stopper and spilled its contents, unnoticed, over his clothes and the uphol-stery. 'I could have told you so!' lamented his wife. 'I've been noticing a sweet smell for some time now. Oh my goodness, a whole flask of *Rosée d'Aurore* completely emptied! I'd been saving it like gold!'

'Why, my dear little silly!' he consoled her, 'don't you see that this was the only way your divine elixir could do us some good? First we were sitting in an oven, and all your fanning was useless. But then suddenly the whole carriage felt cooler. You thought it was because of the few drops I put on my ruffles; we were both revived, and our conversation flowed happily on, when otherwise we should have been hanging our heads like sheep being carted to the slaughter. And we shall be reaping the benefit of this little mishap for the rest of our journey. But come on now, let's stick our two Viennese snouts straight into this green wilderness!'

Arm in arm, they stepped over the ditch at the side of the road, plunging at once into the shade of the pine-trees, which very soon thickened to darkness, sharply broken only here and there by shafts of sunlight that lay across the velvet mossy ground. The refreshing chill, suddenly contrasting with the heat outside, might have proved dangerous to the carefree traveller had his prudent companion not induced him, with some difficulty, to put on the coat which she was holding in readiness.

'My goodness me, what a splendid sight!' he exclaimed, gazing up at the tall tree-trunks. 'You'd think you were in church! I don't believe I've ever been in a forest before, and it never entered my head till now what sort of a thing it is, this whole tribe of trees standing together! No human hand planted them, they all arrived here by themselves, and there they stand, just because they enjoy living and keeping house together. You know, when I was young I used to travel around all over Europe, I've seen the Alps and the sea and all the great and beautiful things of creation: and now by chance here I am, poor simpleton, standing in a pine-wood on the Bohemian border, amazed and enraptured to find that such a thing actually exists and is not merely *una finzione di poeti*, like nymphs and fauns and other things they invent, and not just a stage wood either, but one that has really grown out of the ground, growing tall on moisture and the warmth and light of the sun! This is where the stag lives, with his extraordinary antlers zig-zagging out of his head, and so does the funny little squirrel and the wood-grouse and the jay.'

He stooped down and picked a toadstool, praising its splendid scarlet colour and the delicate white gills on the underside of its cap; he also pocketed an assortment of pine-cones.

'One might think,' remarked his wife, 'that you had never yet taken twenty steps into the Prater, which after all also boasts these rare treasures.'

'Prater forsooth! God bless my soul, what a place to mention here! Nothing but carriages, gentlemen with swords, ladies in all their finery with fans, music, the whole spectacle of high society – how can one ever notice anything else there? And even those trees that give themselves such airs, I don't know – all the beechnuts and acorns that cover the ground, they're scarcely distinguishable from all the corks that have fallen among them, discarded corks from a thousand bottles. Two hours' walk away from the Prater woods and you can still smell waiters and sauces.'

'Oh, hark at him!' she exclaimed, 'that's how he talks now, the man whose chief pleasure's to dine in the Prater on roast chicken!'

When they were both back in the carriage and the road, after running level for a short way, began dipping downwards into a smiling landscape which merged with the hills in the further distance, our maestro was silent for a while and then resumed his theme. 'This earth of ours, you know, is really beautiful, and we can't hold it against any man if

5

he wants to stay on it as long as possible. Thank God I feel as fresh and well as ever, and there are a thousand things I could fancy doing; and sure enough, their turn will come to be done just as soon as my new work has been finished and produced. How much there is out there in the world and how much here at home, how many remarkable and beautiful things of which I still know nothing: wonders of nature, sciences, arts and crafts! That black-faced lad by his charcoal kiln, he knows exactly as much as I do about a whole lot of things, even though I too have a wish and a fancy to take a look at many matters that just don't happen to be in my line of business.'

'The other day,' she replied, 'I found your old pocket diary for the year '85; you'd made three or four jottings at the back, things to remember. The first was "Mid-October: casting of the great bronze lions at the Imperial foundry"; the second, heavily marked: "Visit Professor Gattner!" Who is he?'

'Oh yes, I know – that's the dear old man at the Observatory who invites me there from time to time. I've been wanting to take you along some day to see the moon with me, and the man in the moon. They've got a vast great telescope up there now; they say you can look at the huge disc and see mountains and valleys and ravines, as clear as if you could touch them, and the shadows cast by the mountains from the side the sun doesn't shine on. For two years now I've been meaning to go, and I can't get round to it, to my eternal shame and disgrace!'

'Well,' she replied, 'the moon won't run away. There'll be time to catch up on what we've missed.'

After a pause he went on: 'And isn't that how it always is? Ugh! I can't bear to think how much one misses and puts off and leaves hanging in the air – to say nothing of duties to God and man – I just mean how many of the small innocent pleasures that offer themselves every day of one's life.'

Madame Mozart could see that her husband's lively mood was now increasingly taking a direction from which she was neither able nor willing to divert him, and sadly she could do no more than wholeheartedly agree as with mounting emotion he continued: 'Have I ever even had the pleasure of being with my children for as much as an hour? How half-hearted it always is with me, how fleeting! Lifting the boys up to ride on my knees, chasing about the room with them for a couple of minutes, and *basta*! that's it, down they go again! I can't recall that we've ever made a day of it out in the country together, at Easter or Whitsun, in a garden or a wood or in the fields, just us together, romping around with the little ones and playing with the flowers, just to be back in one's own childhood again. And meanwhile life goes by, it runs and rushes past – Oh, God, once you start on such thoughts, what a sweat of fear you break into!'

With the utterance of these self-reproaches, the intimate and affectionate conversation now developing between the couple had unexpectedly taken a more serious turn. We prefer not to acquaint our

7

reader with its further details, but offer instead a more general survey of the situation which in part, expressly and directly, supplied the theme of their discussion, and in part merely constituted its familiar background.

We must at the outset sadly acknowledge that Mozart, despite his passionate nature, his susceptibility to all the delights of this life and to all that is within the highest reach of the human imagination, and notwithstanding all that he had experienced, enjoyed and created in the short span allotted to him, had nevertheless all his life lacked a stable and untroubled feeling of inner contentment.

Without probing deeper than we need into the causes of this phenomenon, we may in the first instance perhaps find them simply in those habitual and apparently insuperable weaknesses which we so readily, and not without some reason, perceive as somehow necessarily associated with everything in him that we most admire.

His needs were very various, above all his passion for the pleasures of society was extraordinarily strong. Honoured and sought out as an incomparable talent by Vienna's noblest families, he seldom or never declined invitations to dinners, parties and soirées. In addition he would entertain his own circle of friends with befitting hospitality. The Sunday musical evening, a long-established tradition in his house, or the informal luncheon at his well-furnished table with a few friends and acquaintances two or three times a week, were pleasures he refused to forgo. Sometimes, to his wife's dismay, he would bring unannounced guests straight in off the street, a very varied assortment of people, dilettanti, artistic colleagues, singers and poets. The idle parasite whose sole merit lay in an untiring vivacity, ready wit and the coarser sort of humour was made as welcome as the learned connoisseur and the virtuoso musician. For the most part, however, Mozart sought relaxation outside his own home. As often as not he was to be seen playing billiards in a coffee-house after lunch, or passing the evening in a tavern. He was very fond of driving or riding in the country with a party of friends; being an accomplished dancer, he liked going to balls and masquerades, and he particularly enjoyed taking part in popular festivals several times a year, especially the open-air fête on St Bridget's Day, at which he would appear in pierrot costume.

These pleasures, sometimes wild and boisterous and sometimes attuned to a more peaceful mood, served the purpose of giving his creative intellect much-needed rest after its enormous tensions and exertions; and they had the additional and incidental effect, following the mysterious unconscious play of genius, of communicating to it those subtle and fleeting impressions which sometimes quicken it to fruitful activity. But unfortunately it also happened at those times, when it was so important to drain the auspicious moment to its last drop, that no other consideration whether of prudence or of duty, of self-preservation or of good house-keeping, was able to make itself felt. In his creative work as in his pleasures, Mozart exceeded any limit he could set himself. All his nights were partly devoted to composition, which he would revise and finish early next morning, often while still in bed. Then, from ten o'clock onwards, called for on foot or by carriage, he would go the rounds of his lessons, which as a rule would take up some hours of the afternoon as well. 'We're working ourselves to the bone to make an honest living,' he himself once wrote to a patron, 'and often it's hard not to lose patience. One happens to be a well-accredited cembalo player and music teacher, and lo and behold one has a dozen pupils on one's back, and then another and another, no questions asked whether they're any good or not provided they pay cash on the nail. Any old mustachioed Hungarian from the Corps of Engineers is welcome, if Satan has put an itch in him to study ground-bass and counterpoint for no reason whatever; or any conceited little countess who receives me red as a turkeycock if I don't turn up on her doorstep dead on time, as if I were Master Coquerel the coiffeur! . . .' And then, when these and other professional labours, classes, rehearsals and so forth had tired him out and he needed some fresh air to breathe, he would often find that his exhausted nervous system could only be restored to a semblance of life by fresh excitement. All this imperceptibly undermined his health, at least nourishing if not actually causing his recurrent fits of melancholy, and so inevitably fulfilling that premonition of early death which dogged his footsteps to the last. Every kind of anguish, including remorse, was familiar to him like a bitter flavour on all his joys. And yet we know that these sorrows too, purified and serene, all met and mingled in that deep fountain from which they leapt again in a hundred golden streams, as his changing melodies inexhaustibly poured forth all the torment and rapture of the human heart.

The ill-effects of Mozart's way of life were most plainly to be seen in his domestic arrangements. The reproach of foolish, irresponsible extravagance was well merited, and even went hand in hand with one of his most lovable traits of character. A caller who turned up in dire need to ask him for a loan, to beg him to stand surety, had usually calculated in advance that Mozart would not bother to negotiate any terms or guarantee of repayment; and indeed it was no more in his nature than in a child's to do so. He liked best to make an immediate outright gift, and always with laughing generosity, especially when he felt that for the time being he had money to spare.

The expense involved in such lavishness, in addition to ordinary household needs, naturally far exceeded his income. His earnings from theatres and concerts, publishers and pupils, together with his pension from the Emperor, were quite insufficient, if only because his music was still far from commending itself decisively to public taste. The pure beauty, complexity and profundity of Mozart's work were commonly found less palatable than the more easily digestible fare to which his hearers were accustomed. It is true that *Il Seraglio*, thanks to the popular elements in this piece, had in its time so delighted the Viennese that they could scarcely have enough of it. *Figaro*, on the other hand, competing a few years later with the charming but far slighter *Cosa rara*, had been an unexpected and lamentable failure, which was certainly not only due to the Director's intrigues. Yet this very same *Figaro* had then almost at once been received with such enthusiasm by the better educated or less prejudiced audiences of Prague, that the master, touched and grateful, had decided to write his next great opera specially for them.

Notwithstanding the unpropitious times and the influence of his enemies, Mozart might still, if he had exercised a little more circumspection and prudence, have earned a very respectable income by his art. As things were, however, he fell short of success even in those ventures which won him acclamation from the great mass of the public. It seemed, in fact, that fate, his own character and his own weaknesses all conspired to prevent this unique man of genius from prospering and surviving.

We may readily understand with what difficulties a housewife who knew her duty must have been faced in such circumstances. Although herself young and lively, the daughter of a musician and no stranger to artistic temperament, as well as having been brought up to live frugally, Constanze willingly did her utmost to stop the waste at its source, to cut short some of her husband's excesses and make good the large-scale loss by small economies. But it was perhaps in this last respect that she lacked the right skill and experience. It was she who kept the money and the household accounts; every bill, every demand for repayment and all the unpleasantness fell only to her to deal with. Thus there were times when she almost lost heart, especially when these household worries, the privations, the painful embarrassments and the fear of public disgrace, were compounded by her husband's moods of depression, which would over-whelm him for days on end. Idle and inconsolable, he would sit sighing and lamenting beside his wife, or brooding by himself in a corner, and as a screw follows its endless thread, so he would dwell endlessly on the single gloomy theme of his wish to die. Nevertheless her good humour seldom deserted her, and her clear common sense usually stood them in good stead, even if only for a short time. In the essentials there was little or no improvement. Even when she did, with a mixture of seriousness and cajolery, of flattery and plead-ing, succeed in persuading him, just this once, to take tea with her or to enjoy dinner with his family and then spend the evening at home, what good did it do? Occasionally, indeed, noticing with dismay and emotion that his wife had been shedding tears, he would sincerely abjure this or that bad habit, promise complete reform and more than she had asked – it was all in vain, for he would soon slip back into his old ways. It was tempting to believe that to do otherwise was simply not in his power, and that somehow to have forcibly imposed on him a completely different way of life, conforming to our ideas of what is proper and beneficial for mankind generally, would in his case have been the very way to destroy this unique and miraculous individual.

Constanze nevertheless kept on hoping that a favourable turn of events might be brought about by external causes, that is to say by a radical improvement in their financial position, which in view of her husband's growing reputation she fully expected. If only, she thought, the constant pressure could be relieved, the economic pressure which he himself directly or indirectly felt; if only he might follow his true calling undividedly, without having to sacrifice half his strength and his time merely to earn money; and if only he no longer had to chase after his pleasures, but could enjoy them with a far better conscience and with twice the profit for his body and soul! Then indeed his whole state of mind would become easier, more natural, more peaceful. She even planned that they would one day move and live elsewhere, convinced as she was that despite his absolute preference for Vienna there was no real future for him there, and that she might in the end be able to persuade him of this.

But there was now a next, decisive step to be taken towards the realization of Madame Mozart's thoughts and wishes: and this, she hoped, would be the success of the new opera which was the purpose of their present journey.

Its composition was well over halfway completed. Close friends well qualified to judge, who had followed the progress of this extraordinary work and were well placed to form some idea of its character and probable reception, spoke everywhere of it in a tone of such wonderment that even among Mozart's enemies many were prepared to see *Don Giovanni*, before it was six months old, stirring and taking by storm and changing the face of the entire musical world from one end of Germany to the other. Other well-wishers, speaking with greater caution and reserve, based their forecasts on the present state of musical fashion, and were less hopeful of a general and rapid success. The maestro himself privately shared their only too well-founded scepticism.

Constanze for her part, like any woman of lively temperament and especially when her feelings are dominated by an entirely understandable wish, was much less susceptible than men to such misgivings and second thoughts of one kind or another, and held fast to her hopeful view, which indeed, now in the carriage, she yet again had occasion to defend. She did so in her most charming and high-spirited manner and with redoubled energy, for Mozart had become noticeably more depressed in the course of their foregoing talk, which of course had been quite inconclusive and had broken off in deep dissatisfaction. Still full of good humour, she explained in detail to her husband how, when they got home, she proposed to spend the hundred ducats for which they had agreed to sell the score of the opera to the Prague impresario: it would cover the most urgent items of debt as well as some other expenses, and she had good hopes of managing on her household budget through the winter and into the spring.

'Your Signor Bondini,' she declared, 'will be feathering his nest on your opera, you may be sure of that; and if he is even half the man of honour you keep saying he is, he'll be paying you back a tidy percentage from the royalties he'll get for copies of the score from one theatre after another. And if not, well then, thank God, we have other possibilities in prospect, and much sounder ones too. I can foresee quite a few things.'

'Let's hear about them.'

'The other day a little bird told me that the King of Prussia needs a new Kapellmeister.'

'Oho!'

'Director-General of Music, I should say. Let me have my little daydream! It's a weakness I inherited from my mother.'

'Dream away; the crazier the better!'

'No no, it's all quite sane. First, let's assume – in a year's time, let us say –'

'On the Pope's wedding-day –'

'Oh do be quiet! I predict that in a year come St Giles there will no longer be any Imperial court composer answering to the name of Wolf Mozart.'

'Well now, devil take you, my dear.'

'I can already hear our old friends gossiping about us, telling each other all sorts of stories.'

'For instance?'

'One morning, for instance, our old admirer General Volkstett's wife comes sailing straight across the Kohlmarkt soon after nine o'clock on a visiting expedition, all on fire after three months' absence: she has finally made that great journey to her brother-in-law in Saxony that she's chattered about daily ever since we first met her. She got back last night, and now her heart is full to bursting – fairly brimming over with happy travel memories and impatience to see her friends and delightful titbits of news to tell them – and off she rushes to the Colonel's wife with it all! Up the stairs she storms and knocks on the door and doesn't wait for a "Come in". Just picture the jubilation and the huggings and kisses! "Well, my dearest Madame Colonel," she begins, when she's caught her breath again after the preliminaries, "I've brought you a multitude of greetings, just guess from whom! I didn't come straight back from Stendal, we made a little detour, we took a left turn to Brandenburg." "What! Is it possible? You went to Berlin? You've been visiting the Mozarts?" "For ten lovely days!" "Oh my sweet, my dear, my darling Madame General, tell me about it, describe them! How are our dear young friends? Are they still as happy there as they were at first? I find it so extraordinary, unthinkable, even now, and all the more now that you've just been to see him – Mozart a Berliner! How is he behaving? How does he look?" "Oh, him! You should just see him. This summer the King sent him to Carlsbad. Can you imagine his best-beloved Emperor Joseph thinking of that, eh? The two of them had only just got back when I arrived. He's aglow with health and energy, he's round and plump and lively as quicksilver, with happiness and contentment just written all over his face."'

And now Constanze, speaking in her assumed role, began to paint her husband's new situation in glowing colours. From his apartment in Unter den Linden, his country house and garden, to the brilliant scenes of his public activity and the intimate Court circles where he would be invited to accompany the Queen on the piano: all this seemed to become real and vividly present in her descriptions. Whole conversations and delightful anecdotes came tumbling out of her as if by magic. She truly seemed more familiar with the Prussian capital, with Potsdam and Sanssouci, than with the Imperial palaces of Vienna and Schönbrunn. She was also roguish enough to endow the person of our hero with a good number of quite new domestic virtues which had supposedly grown and prospered on the solid Prussian soil, and among which our friend Madame Volkstett had noticed above all, as a phenomenon proving how often *les*

extrêmes se touchent, a most wholesome parsimonious tendency which suited him wonderfully well.
'"Yes, just think, he gets his three thousand thalers cash down, and all for what? For conducting a chamber concert once a week and the grand opera twice – oh, dearest Madame Colonel, I saw him, saw our dear little treasure of a man, with his superb orchestra all round him, the orchestra he trained and that worships him! I was sitting with his wife in their box, almost opposite the royal family! And what, I ask you, what was on the programme? – I brought one for you, I've wrapped up a little present in it from the Mozarts and myself – here it is, look, read it, it's printed in letters a yard long!" "What? Heaven help us! *Tarare!*" "Yes, you see, my dear; who would have thought it! Two years ago, when Mozart wrote *Don Giovanni*, that accursed, poisonous Salieri, all black and yellow with envy, was already plotting in secret to repeat the triumph he had in Paris with his own opera, to repeat it without delay on home ground. There was our dear Viennese public, dining on woodsnipe and listening to nothing but *Cosa rara*; well, now he would show them another kind of bird too. So now he and his accomplices were whispering together, planning subtle ways of producing *Don Giovanni* with its feathers well plucked, bald and bare as *Figaro* had been and neither dead nor alive – well, do you know, I made a vow that if that man's infamous opera reached the stage, nothing would induce me to go to it, nothing! And

I kept my word. When everyone was running along to see it – you too, my dear Madame Colonel! – I sat on by my stove with my cat on my lap, eating my pastry-cake; and I did the same thing the next few times it was given. But now, just think: *Tarare* at the Berlin Opera, the work of his arch-enemy, conducted by Mozart! 'You must go to it!' he exclaimed before we'd been talking a quarter of an hour, 'even if it's only so that you can tell them in Vienna that I didn't harm his precious brain-child. I wish he were here himself, the envious pig, and he'd see that I don't need to ruin another man's work in order to prove that I still am what I am!'''

'*Brava, bravissima!*' shouted Mozart, and took his little wife by the ears, and kissed and cuddled and tickled her, until her fanciful game, the many-coloured dreams that floated from her imagination of a future that would, alas, never even begin to be realized, came to an end in high-spirited, mischievous caresses and laughter.

Meanwhile they had been continuing their descent into the valley and were approaching a village which they had already seen from the top of the hill; just beyond it, in the charming plain, was a small country mansion of modern appearance, the residence of a certain Count von Schinzberg. They were planning to feed the horses, rest and have lunch in this village. The inn where they pulled up stood at the end of it by itself on the main road, from one side of which a poplar avenue not six hundred paces long led to the castle grounds.

When they had alighted from the coach, Mozart as usual left it to his wife to order lunch. In the meantime he ordered a glass of wine for himself in the parlour downstairs, while she asked only for a drink of cold water and some quiet corner where she might sleep for an hour. She was shown upstairs, and her husband followed, merrily singing and whistling to himself. The room was white-washed and had been quickly aired. In it, among other old furnishings of finer origin which had no doubt found their way here at one time or another from the castle, stood a clean and elegant four-poster bed with a painted canopy resting on slender green-lacquered columns. Its silk curtains had long ago been replaced with a commoner material. Constanze made herself comfortable, he promised to wake her in good time, she bolted the door behind him, and he now went to seek his own entertainment in the public parlour. There was however no one there except the landlord, and his guest, finding that neither the man's conversation nor his wine was much to his taste, indicated that he would like to take a short walk towards the castle until lunch was ready. The park, he was told, was open to respectable visitors, and in any case the family was not at home today.

He set off and soon covered the short distance to the open park gates, then strolled along an avenue of tall old lime-trees, at the end of which, a little way to the left, the front of the house suddenly came into view. It was built in the Italian style, its walls washed in a light colour and with a double flight of steps grandly projecting from the entrance; the slate roof was decorated with some statues of gods and goddesses in the usual manner and with a balustrade. Our maestro, passing between two large and still profusely blossoming flower beds, walked towards the shadier parts of the garden; he made his way past some groups of beautiful dark pines, along a tangle of winding paths and into the more sunlit areas again, where he followed the lively sound of leaping water and at once found himself standing by a fountain.

The pool was imposingly wide, oval in shape and surrounded by a carefully tended display of orange-trees growing in tubs, which alternated with laurels and oleanders; round them ran a soft sanded pathway, and opening on to this was a little trellised summerhouse which offered a most inviting resting place. A small table stood in front of the bench, and here, near the entrance, Mozart sat down.

As he listened contentedly to the plashing of the fountain and rested his eyes on an orange-tree of medium height, hung with splendid fruit, which stood by itself outside the circle and quite close to him, this glimpse of the warm south at once led our friend's thoughts to a delightful recollection of his own boyhood. With a pensive smile he reached out to the nearest orange, as if to feel its magnificent rounded shape and succulent coolness in the hollow of his hand. But closely interwoven with that scene from his youth as it reappeared before his mind's eye was a long-forgotten musical memory, and for a while his reverie followed its uncertain trace. By now his eyes were alight and straying to and fro: he was seized by an idea, which he immediately and eagerly pursued. Unthinkingly he again grasped the orange, which came away from its branch and dropped into his hand. He saw this happen and yet did not see it; indeed so far did the distraction of his creative mood take him as he sat there twirling the scented fruit from side to side under his nose, while his lips silently toyed with a melody, beginning and continuing and beginning it again, that he finally, instinctively, brought out an enamelled sheath from his side pocket, took from it a small silver-handled knife, and slowly cut through the yellow globe of the orange from top to bottom. He had perhaps been moved by an obscure impulse of thirst, yet his excited senses were content merely to breathe in the fruit's exquisite fragrance. For some moments he gazed at its two inner surfaces, then joined them gently, very gently together, parted them and reunited them again.

At this point he heard footsteps approaching and was startled into sudden awareness of where he was and what he had done. He was about to try to hide the orange, but stopped at once, either from pride or because it was too late anyway. Before him stood a tall broad-shouldered man in livery, the head gardener of the estate. This fellow had no doubt observed the suspicious movement Mozart had just made, and was momentarily lost for words. The composer, also speechless and evidently riveted to his seat, stared half laughingly, visibly blushing yet with a certain impudence, straight up into the man's face with his great blue eyes; and then – an onlooker would have found this very comical – he set the seemingly undamaged orange with a bold, defiant and emphatic gesture down in the centre of the table.

'Excuse me,' began the gardener with barely concealed annoyance, after taking a look at the inauspicious dress of the stranger, 'I do not know whom I have the –'

'Kapellmeister Mozart from Vienna.'

'No doubt, sir, you are known to the family?'

'I am a stranger here and on my way through. Is his lordship at home?'

'No.'

'Her ladyship?'

'Her ladyship is busy and not receiving visitors.'

Mozart rose to his feet and turned to go.

'By your leave, sir – may I ask by what right you simply come in here and help yourself like this?'

'What?' exclaimed Mozart, 'help myself? Devil take it, man, do you think I meant to steal this thing here and eat it?'

'Sir, I think what my eyes tell me. These oranges have been counted and I am responsible for them. His lordship selected this tree specially for use at an entertainment, it is just about to be taken to the house. I cannot let you go until I have reported the matter and you have given your explanation of how this happened.'

'Very well. I shall wait here until you do that. You can depend on it, my good fellow!'

The gardener looked about him with some hesitation, and Mozart, thinking that perhaps a tip might settle the matter, put his hand in his pocket, only to find that he had not a penny in his possession.

They were in fact now joined by two under-gardeners, who loaded the tree on to a hurdle and carried it away. In the meantime the maestro had taken out his pocketbook, extracted a sheet of paper, and with the gardener still standing over him had begun to pencil the following lines:

Most gracious Lady,

Here I sit, poor wretch, in your paradise, like our forefather Adam after he had tasted the apple. The damage is already done, and I cannot even shift the blame for it to my dear Eve, who at this very moment, with the graces and amoretti of her canopied bed fluttering round her, lies at the inn enjoying the sweet sleep of innocence. Command me, and I will personally answer to your Ladyship for a misdeed which I myself find incomprehensible. In sincere mortification

Your Ladyship's most humble servant
W. A. Mozart,
en route to Prague.

Folding up the note rather clumsily, he handed it to the servant, who was still waiting uneasily, and told him to deliver it as directed.

No sooner had the enemy withdrawn than a carriage was heard entering the courtyard at the back of the castle. It was the Count bringing home his niece and her fiancé, a rich young baron, from the neighbouring estate. Since the Baron's mother had for years been confined to her house, today's betrothal ceremony had taken place there, and now an additional happy celebration, with a number of relatives invited, was to be held at the castle, for it was here that Eugenie, whom the Count and Countess treated like a daughter, had found a second home since her childhood. The Countess and her son, Lieutenant Max, had returned a little earlier to make various arrangements, and the whole house was now a hive of activity upstairs and downstairs, so that it was only with difficulty that the gardener at last managed to hand the note to the Countess in the anteroom; she however, paying little attention to what the messenger said, did not open it at once but went hastily about her affairs. He waited and waited, but she did not return. One after another of the servants, valets and lady's maids and footmen, hurried past him. He asked for the Count and was told that his lordship was busy changing his clothes. Then he looked for Count Max, but he was deep in conversation with the Baron, and fearing that the gardener was about to make some inquiry or announcement which would prematurely reveal something about the evening's plans, cut him short as he spoke: 'Yes, yes, I'm coming, off you go now.' Some time passed before the father and son eventually appeared together and received the painful news.

'Why, damnation take it!' exclaimed the good-natured, stout but somewhat irascible Count, 'that's absolutely intolerable! A musician from Vienna, you say? Some sort of tramp, I suppose, wandering about begging for alms and grabbing whatever he can find?'

'By your leave, my lord, that is not quite what he seems to be. I think he's not right in the head. And he's very arrogant. He says his name is Moser. He's down there waiting to hear from us. I told Franz to stay near by and keep an eye on him.'

'What's the point of that now, damn it! Even if I have the fool locked up, the damage can't be repaired. I've told you over and over again that the main gate must always be kept shut. But the mischief would have been prevented anyway if you'd taken proper precautions sooner.'

At this point the Countess, with Mozart's note open in her hand and in a great state of joyful excitement, hurried in from the adjoining room. 'Who do you think is in our garden?' she cried. 'For God's sake, read this letter – it's Mozart from Vienna, the composer! We must go down at once and invite him in – if only he hasn't left already! What will he think of me! I hope you treated him politely, Velten? Whatever happened?'

'Happened?' retorted her husband, whose annoyance could not be immediately and completely assuaged even by the prospect of a visit from such a celebrity. 'Why, the crazy fellow has picked one of the nine oranges off that tree I was keeping for Eugenie! It's monstrous! This means that the whole point of our little pleasantry has been spoilt, and Max may as well scrap his poem straight away!'

'Oh, nonsense!' insisted his wife. 'The gap can be filled easily, just leave it to me. Go to him now, the two of you, release the dear man and make him welcome, as kindly and flatteringly as you can! He shall not travel any further today if we can possibly keep him here. If you don't find him still in the garden, look for him at the inn and bring him back with his wife. What a splendid present, what a wonderful surprise for Eugenie, on this day of all days! There couldn't have been a happier chance.'

'Certainly!' replied Max. 'That was my first thought too. Quick, Papa, come along!' And as they hurried out and down the steps, he added: 'You can set your mind at rest about the lines. The ninth Muse shall not be the loser; on the contrary, I shall turn this mishap to particular advantage.'

'Impossible!'

'Most certainly!'

'Well, if that is so – but I'll have to take your word for it – let us find this strange fellow and do him all the honour we can.'

While this was happening at the castle, our quasi-prisoner, not greatly concerned about the

28

outcome of the incident, had sat on for some time writing busily. But since no one appeared, he began to pace uneasily to and fro; and now, too, an urgent message came for him from the inn to say that lunch was ready and waiting, that he must please come at once, that the postilion was anxious to continue the journey. And so he gathered his things together and was just about to leave without further ado, when the two gentlemen appeared outside the summerhouse.

The Count greeted him heartily in his loud booming voice, almost as if he were an old friend, cutting short all his attempts to offer an apology, and at once expressing his wish to have both Mozart and his wife spend at least this afternoon and this evening with him and his family. 'My dearest Maestro,' he declared, 'you are so far from being a stranger to us that I may say I know of no other place in which the name of Mozart is mentioned more often or with more fervent admiration than here. My niece sings and plays, she spends almost her entire day at the piano, knows your works by heart, and it has been her dearest wish that one day she might see you at closer quarters than was possible last winter at that concert of yours she went to. We are going to Vienna for a few weeks before long, and her relations have promised her an invitation to Prince Galitzin's where you are often to be found. But now you are going to Prague, you'll be staying there for some time and God knows whether your return journey will bring you our way again. Give yourself a holiday today and tomorrow! We can send your carriage back at once, and if you will permit me I shall take care of the rest of your journey.'

The composer, well used to making much greater sacrifices to friendship or pleasure than the Count's invitation involved, very gladly accepted his hospitality for the rest of the day, on the understanding that he must resume his journey early the following morning. Count Max requested the pleasure of fetching Madame Mozart from the inn himself and of making all the necessary arrangements there. He set off on foot, giving instructions for a carriage to follow him immediately.

We should remark in passing that this young man combined the happy temperament he had inherited from his father and mother with a talent and enthusiasm for intellectual pursuits, and although military life was not really to his taste, he had also distinguished himself as an officer by his wide knowledge and good education. He was well read in French literature, and at a time when German poetry was not very highly regarded in fashionable circles, he had won praise and favour by writing in his native tongue, using the poetic forms with considerable facility and deriving them from good models such as Hagedorn, Götz and others. Today, as we have already heard, he had been presented with a particularly agreeable opportunity to make use of his gift.

Madame Mozart, when he arrived, was sitting

at the laid table chattering to the innkeeper's daughter, and had already helped herself in advance to a bowl of soup. She was too well accustomed to unusual incidents and bold impromptu behaviour by her husband to be unduly surprised by the young officer's arrival or the message he brought. With undisguised pleasure, and using all her good sense and competence, she at once discussed and took charge of the needful arrangements. The luggage was repacked, the bill paid, the postilion dismissed; and making herself ready without too much anxious attention to her toilet, she drove in high spirits with her escort to the castle, little suspecting how strange her husband's introduction to it had been.

He in the meantime was already very contentedly installed there and enjoying the best of entertainment. It was not long before he met Eugenie and her fiancé. She was a most graceful, sensitive girl in the flower of youth: blonde, slender, festively dressed in lustrous crimson silk trimmed with costly lace, and wearing round her brow a white fillet set with splendid pearls. The Baron, only a little older than his bride, was of a gentle and open disposition and seemed worthy of her in every way.

The first and almost too generous contributor to the conversation was the genial and temperamental master of the house himself, whose rather boisterous manner of speaking was plentifully larded with jests and anecdotes. Refreshments were served, and our traveller did them full justice.

Someone had opened the piano, the score of *The Marriage of Figaro* was lying there ready, and the young lady, accompanied by the Baron, was about to sing Susanna's aria in the garden scene – that aria in which the very essence of sweet passion seems to pour into us with the fragrant air of the summer night. The delicate flush on Eugenie's cheeks gave way for a moment to extreme pallor; but with the first melodious note her lips uttered, all the bonds of diffidence dropped from her heart. She moved smilingly and effortlessly along the high wave of the music, inspired by this moment which was surely one that she would treasure as unique for the rest of her life.

Mozart was clearly taken by surprise. When she had finished he approached her and spoke in his artlessly sincere manner: 'My dear child, what can I say? You are like the sun in the sky, which sings its own praises best by shining and warming us all! When one's soul hears singing like that, it feels like a baby in its bath: it laughs, it is amazed, it has not another wish in the world. And believe me: hearing one's own music rendered with such purity, such simplicity and warmth, indeed with such completeness – that's not a thing that happens to one every day in Vienna!' And so saying he took her hand and kissed it affectionately. Eugenie was so overwhelmed by his great charm and kindness, to say nothing of the honour he did to her talent with such a compliment, that she came near to fainting, and her eyes filled suddenly with tears.

At this point Mozart's wife arrived, and soon after her came new and expected guests: a baronial family, neighbours and close relations, whose daughter Francesca had been Eugenie's bosom friend since childhood and knew the castle as her second home. Greetings, embraces and congratulations were exchanged all round, the two visitors from Vienna were introduced, and Mozart sat down at the piano. He played part of one of his own concertos, one which Eugenie happened to be studying at the time.

The effect of such a recital in a small circle of this kind is naturally distinguished from any given in a public place by the infinite satisfaction of immediate personal contact with the artist and his genius in a familiar domestic setting. The concerto was one of those brilliant pieces in which pure beauty, as if by gratuitous choice, freely submits to the service of elegance, but in such a way as to seem merely disguised by the exuberant play of forms, merely hidden behind a myriad dazzling points of light: for in its every movement it discloses its own essential nobility and pours forth its own passionate splendour in rich profusion.

The Countess privately observed that most of the small audience and perhaps even Eugenie herself, despite the rapt concentration and reverent silence with which they listened to so enchanting a performance, were nevertheless very much in two minds between listening and watching. With one's eyes involuntarily drawn to the composer, to his simple, almost rigid posture, his kindly face, the rounded movement of those small hands, it must have been scarcely possible to dispel from one's mind a whole complex of conflicting thoughts about this miraculous prodigy.

When the master had risen to his feet again, the Count turned to Madame Mozart and said: 'How lucky the kings and emperors are! It's no easy matter, you know, to meet a famous artist and praise him as a wit and a connoisseur should. But in a royal mouth, anything at all sounds pointed and remarkable. What liberties they can take! How easy it would be, for example, to come right up behind your good husband's chair, and at the final chord of some brilliant fantasy to give the modest classical master a clap on the shoulder and say "My dear Mozart, you are a hell of a fellow!" The word would no sooner be spoken than it would go round the room like wildfire: "What did he say to him?" "He said he was a hell of a fellow!" And all the fiddlers and pipers and music-makers would be beside themselves at this one phrase. In short, that's the grand style, the inimitable homely imperial style I've always envied in the Josephs and Fredericks of this world, and never more than at this moment. For may the devil take me if I can find in all my pockets even the smallest coin of any other compliment to pay him!'

The roguish manner of the Count's speech was well enough received, and the company could not help laughing. Now, however, at their hostess's invitation, they proceeded to the richly decorated circular dining-room, where a festive scent of flowers greeted them and a cooler air sharpened their appetite as they entered.

Places at table were suitably allocated and the company sat down, the guest of honour finding himself opposite the bridal pair. As neighbours he had on one side an elderly little lady, an unmarried aunt of Francesca, and on the other the charming young Francesca herself, who quickly captivated him by her intelligence and gaiety. Madame Constanze sat between their host and her obliging escort the Lieutenant, and the rest disposed themselves appropriately, making a party of eleven, with the sexes alternating as nearly as possible, and the lower end of the table left empty. In the middle were two enormous porcelain centrepieces with painted figures holding up large bowls heaped with natural fruit and flowers. Magnificent festoons hung on the walls. The remaining provisions already served or following in due course were appropriate to a prolonged banquet. Noble wines stood ready between the dishes and plates or gleamed from the sideboard, a whole variety ranging from the deepest red to the pale gold with its merry foam that is traditionally kept back to crown the latter half of a feast.

Until about this time the conversation, in which a number of lively participants joined, had been flowing in all directions. From the outset, however, the Count had several times alluded, at first obliquely but then ever more directly and boldly, to Mozart's adventure in the garden; and since some of those present reacted to this only with a discreet smile, while others were vainly racking their brains to guess what he might be talking about, our friend felt it was incumbent upon him to address the company.

'Since I needs must,' he began, 'I will confess how it was that I had the honour of becoming acquainted with this noble house. It is a story that does me little credit, and but for the grace of God I should now be sitting, not at this very happy table, but on an empty stomach in some remote dungeon of his lordship's castle, counting the cobwebs on the walls.'

'Goodness me!' exclaimed Constanze, 'now I shall hear some fine story!'

Whereupon Mozart described in detail first how he had left his wife behind in the White Horse, his walk in the park, then the calamity in the arbour, his confrontation with the garden constabulary, in short the facts more or less as we already know them, narrating them all with the greatest candour and to the extreme delight of his audience. Their hilarity was almost unstoppable, and even the quiet Eugenie could not refrain, but simply shook with laughter.

'Well,' he continued, 'as they say, bad luck like this never comes amiss! The affair has stood me in good stead, as you shall see. But first of all let me tell you how it came about that a silly fellow like me could so forget himself. It came about partly because of a memory from my childhood.

'In the spring of 1770, as a little boy of thirteen, I travelled to Italy with my father. From Rome we went to Naples. I had played twice at the Conservatoire there and at several other places as well. The nobility and clergy showed us great kindness; in particular a certain Abbé attached himself to us, who took pride in being something of a connoisseur and was also well connected at Court. The day before we left, he took us with some other gentlemen to a royal garden, the Villa Reale, which runs along the fine boulevard by the seashore. A troupe of Sicilian actors was performing – *figli di Nettuno* they called themselves, as well as various other fancy names. There we were, with many distinguished onlookers, among them the charming young Queen Carolina herself with two princesses. We were sitting on a long row of benches, shaded by the tent-like canopy of a low loggia with the waves lapping against the terrace below it. The sea was ribboned with many different colours, reflecting the splendid blue sky. Straight ahead was Vesuvius, with the gentle curve of the lovely shimmering coastline to our left.

'The first part of the performance was over; it was given on the dry wooden boards of a kind of raft moored offshore, and there was nothing specially remarkable about it. But the second and most beautiful part consisted entirely of boating and swimming and diving displays, and it has remained in my memory ever since, fresh in every detail.

'Two vessels, elegant and very lightly built, were approaching each other from opposite directions, each of them seemingly on a pleasure trip. One of them was slightly larger, it had a half deck and rowing benches, but also a slender mast and a sail; it was splendidly painted, with a gilded prow. On board, five conventionally handsome and scantily clad youths, their arms, legs and chests apparently naked, were either rowing or disporting themselves with an equal number of attractive girls who were their sweethearts. One of these, sitting in the middle of the deck weaving garlands of flowers, was taller and more beautiful as well as more richly adorned than the rest of them. The latter were willingly serving her, spreading an awning to shelter her from the sun and handing her flowers from the basket. Another girl sat at her feet playing a flute, accompanying the singing of the others with its bright tones. This exceptional beauty also had her own particular protector; but the two of them behaved to each other with a certain indifference, and her lover almost seemed to me to be treating her rather roughly.

'In the meantime the other, plainer vessel had drawn nearer. The young people in it were all male. The colour worn by the boys in the first ship was scarlet, and these were in sea-green. Their attention was caught by the sight of the pretty girls; they waved greetings to them and signalled that they desired their closer acquaintance. The liveliest of the girls now took a rose from her breast and held it up coquettishly, as if asking whether such gifts would be acceptable, to which the others replied with unambiguous gestures. The red youths looked on scornfully and angrily, but there was nothing they could do when some of the girls decided at least to throw the poor devils something to satisfy their hunger and thirst. There was a basket of oranges standing on the deck; probably they were only yellow balls made to look like the fruit. And now an enchanting spectacle started, accompanied by music from the players on the quayside.

'One of the maidens began by lightly tossing a few oranges across, which were caught with equal dexterity and at once thrown back; and thus it continued to and fro, with gradually more and more of the girls taking part, until oranges by the dozen were flying hither and thither at ever-increasing speed. The beautiful girl in the middle took neither side in this contest, merely watching eagerly from her seat. We were lost in admiration for the skill shown by both parties. The two boats circled each other slowly, about thirty paces apart, sometimes lying broadside on, sometimes aslant with bows converging. About twenty-four balls were constantly in the air, but in the confusion there seemed to be many more of them. At times a regular crossfire developed, and often they rose and fell in a high curving trajectory. Only a very few missed their mark, for as if by some power of attraction they fell of their own accord straight into the grasping fingers.

'But delightful though all this was as a spectacle for the eye, our hearing was equally charmed by the accompanying melodies: Sicilian airs, dances, *saltarelli, canzoni a ballo*, a whole medley of pieces lightly interwoven with each other like garlands. The younger princess, a sweet innocent creature of about my age, was nodding her head very nicely in time to the music; to this day I can still see her smile and her long eyelashes.

'Now let me briefly tell you how this comedy continued, although it is not relevant to my theme! It really was the prettiest thing you could imagine. While the skirmishing was gradually coming to an end and only a few more missiles were being exchanged, as the girls collected their golden apples and returned them to the basket, a boy in the other boat, as if in play, had seized a large net of green cords and held it for a short time under water; then he lifted it out, and to everyone's astonishment it had caught a great fish of shimmering colours, blue and green and gold. The others eagerly leapt up to him to pull the fish out, but it slipped out of their hands as if it were really alive, and dropped back into the sea. Now this was an agreed stratagem to fool the red youths and entice them out of their ship. They, as if bewitched by this miracle, had no sooner noticed that the animal did not attempt to dive but continued to play on the surface, than without a moment's hesitation they all hurled themselves into the sea; the green youths did the same, and thus we saw twelve fine-looking expert swimmers, all intent on catching the fleeing fish, which danced about on the waves, disappeared beneath them for minutes on end, and then surfaced again, now here and now there, now between the legs of one of the youths and now between the breast and chin of another. Suddenly, just as the red swimmers were most passionately absorbed in their chase, the other party spied its advantage, and quick as lightning climbed aboard their opponents' vessel, on which the only persons left were the girls, who now set up a great shrieking. The noblest-looking of the boys, who was like the god Mercury in stature, sped straight up to the chief beauty and embraced and kissed her, his face aglow with joy; and she, far from joining in the cries of the others, likewise passionately flung her arms round the neck of this youth, whom she evidently knew well. The other group, thus outwitted, at once came swimming alongside, but were driven off with oars and weapons. Their futile rage, the maidens' startled shrieks, the strenuous resistance of some of them, their pleas and entreaties – all this noise, almost drowned by that of the waves and the music, which had suddenly changed its character – it was all beautiful beyond description, and the audience burst into a storm of enthusiastic applause.

'Now at this moment the sail, hitherto loosely furled, opened out and released from its midst a rosy-cheeked boy with silver wings, with a bow and arrows and quiver, who hovered freely above the mast in a graceful posture. Already all the oars were being plied and the sail was swelling, but the presence of the god and his energetic forward gesture seemed to drive the vessel on more powerfully than either, so much so that the swimmers, in almost breathless pursuit, and with one of them holding the golden fish with his left hand high above his head, soon gave up in exhaustion and were forced to take refuge on the abandoned ship. In the meantime their green opponents had reached a little wooded peninsula, from behind which a handsome vessel full of armed comrades suddenly appeared. With such a threat confronting them, the first group ran up a white flag to signal that they were prepared to negotiate amicably. Encouraged by a similar signal from the other side, they put in at the same landing-place, and soon we saw the good-natured girls, all except the leading one who voluntarily stayed behind, happily going aboard their own ship with their lovers. And that was the end of this comedy.'

There was a short pause in which everyone greeted the narrative with acclamation, and Eugenie, her eyes shining with excitement, whispered to the Baron: 'Surely what we have just been given is a whole symphony in colour from beginning to end, as well as a perfect allegory of the Mozartian genius itself in all its joy and serenity! Am I not right? Does it not embody all the grace of *Figaro*?'

Her fiancé was just about to repeat her remark to the composer when the latter began speaking again.

'It's seventeen years now since I saw Italy. What man who has seen it, and seen Naples above all, does not remember it for the rest of his life, even if, like myself, he was still half a child at the time! But scarcely ever have I experienced so vivid a recollection of that beautiful evening by the Gulf as today, in your garden. Every time I closed my eyes, there it was – quite plain and clear and bright, its last veil lifting and drifting away, that heavenly panorama spread out before me! The sea and the sea-shore, the mountain and the city, the motley crowd of people on the embankment, and then that wonderful complicated game with the balls! My ears seemed to hear that same music again, a whole rosary of happy melodies, some my own and some by others, all and sundry, all following on from each other! Suddenly a little dancing song jumped out, a motif in six-eight time, quite new to me. "Hang on!" I thought, "what's this? Now that's a devilish neat little thing!" I took a closer look, and – good God above, it's Masetto and it's Zerlina!' And he looked laughingly across at Madame Mozart, who at once understood him.

'The fact is simply this,' he continued. 'In the first act of my opera there's an easy little number which I hadn't yet written: a duet and chorus for a country wedding. Two months ago, you see, when it was the turn of this piece to be composed,

43

I couldn't get it right first time round. A simple, childlike melody, bubbling over with happiness, like a fresh posy of flowers and a fluttering ribbon fastened to the girl's dress: that was what I needed. But because one must never try to force anything, and because trifles of this kind often simply write themselves, I just passed it by, and scarcely gave it another thought as I carried on with the main work. Quite fleetingly, as I sat in the carriage today, just before we drove into the village, I remembered the text of that song; but no musical idea developed from it, at least not so far as I know. In fact, only an hour later, in that arbour by the fountain, I picked up a happier and better tune than I could ever have invented at any other time and in any other way. In art one sometimes has strange experiences, but I had never known a trick like that before. For lo and behold, a melody, fitting the line of words like a glove – but let me not anticipate, we're not quite there yet. The little bird had only just stuck its head out of the egg, and at once I began to scoop it out clean and complete. As I did so, I clearly saw Zerlina dancing there before my eyes, and in a strange way that laughing landscape of the Gulf of Naples was there as well. I could hear the voices of the bride and the groom turn about, and the lasses and lads singing in chorus.'

And at this point Mozart began merrily trilling the opening lines of the song:

'Giovinette, che fate all' amore, che fate all' amore,
Non lasciate che passi l'età, che passi l'età, che passi
   l'età!
Se nel seno vi bulica il core, vi bulica il core,
Il remedio vedetelo quà! La la la! La la la!
Che piacer, che piacer che sarà!
Ah la la! Ah la la!' etc.

'Meanwhile, my hands had done the great mischief.
Nemesis was already lying in wait for me just round
the hedge, and now it stepped forth in the guise
of that terrible man in braided blue livery. An erup-
tion of Vesuvius, if it had really occurred on that
divine evening by the sea, and had suddenly smoth-
ered and buried the spectators and actors and the
whole Parthenopean splendour in a black rain of
ashes: by God, it would not have been a more unexpected and dreadful catastrophe than this. Devil
take him! I can't recall when any man has ever put
me in such a pother. A face that might have been
cast in bronze – rather like the cruel Roman
emperor Tiberius! If that's what the servant's like,
I thought after he had left, how am I to look his
lordship himself in the eye! And yet, to tell the
truth, I was even now rather relying on the protec-
tion of the ladies, and not without some reason.
For my little wife Connie here, who's a trifle nosy
by nature, had already in my presence made the
fat woman at the inn tell us most of what we
needed to know about this noble family and all its
members; I was standing there and heard –'

Here Madame Mozart could not refrain from interrupting, and assured the company most emphatically that on the contrary, it was he who had asked all the questions: this gave rise to a good-natured disputation between husband and wife, which caused much amusement. 'Be that as it may,' he declared, 'the fact is that I heard some story somehow about a dear adopted daughter who was engaged to be married, and not only beautiful but kindness itself, and with a voice like an angel. And the thought came to me now: *Per Dio!* that will help me out of my pickle! I'll sit down straight away and write that little song as far as it goes, then I'll give a truthful account of my foolish prank, and the whole thing will be a great joke. No sooner said than done! I had time enough, and even a clean sheet of green-lined paper on me. And here is the result! I lay it in this lady's fair hands – an impromptu bridal song, if you will allow it to count as such.'

So saying, he handed his meticulously written manuscript across the table to Eugenie, but her uncle's hand anticipated hers: he snatched it up, exclaiming: 'Have patience just a moment, my dear!'

At a sign from him the double doors of the dining-room opened wide, and a procession of servants appeared, quietly and ceremoniously carrying in the fateful orange-tree and setting it down on a bench at the end of the table; at the same time two slender myrtles were placed to the left and right of it. An inscription fastened to the trunk of the orange-tree declared it to be the property of the bride; but in front of it, on the surrounding moss, stood a porcelain plate covered with a napkin. When this was removed, an orange cut into two halves was revealed, and beside it on the plate, with a meaningful look, Eugenie's uncle laid the master's autograph. All this was greeted by the company with prolonged and tumultuous applause.

'I really think,' said the Countess, 'that Eugenie still does not even know what is standing there before her. I'll wager she doesn't recognize her beloved old tree in its new glory and all covered with fruit!'

Startled and unable to believe her eyes, the young lady looked from the tree to her uncle and back again. 'It's not possible!' she said. 'I know it was so far gone that it couldn't be saved.'

'So you think, do you,' he replied, 'that we just picked up some kind of substitute to present to you? That would have been a fine compliment! No, just take a look at this – now I have to do what they do in comedies, when long-lost sons or brothers have to prove their identity by birthmarks and scars. Look at this lump! and this crack where the branches divide – you must have noticed it a hundred times. Well now: is it, or isn't it?' And she could doubt it no longer; her amazement, her emotion and her joy were indescribable.

For the family, this tree was associated with a memory that went back more than a hundred years, the memory of a great lady, who well deserves that we should give a brief account of her here.

The grandfather of Eugenie's uncle, whose diplomatic accomplishments had won him honour in the Imperial ministry and who had enjoyed the equal trust of two successive rulers, was no less fortunate in his domestic affairs as the husband of an excellent wife, Renate Leonore. Her repeated visits to France brought her into frequent contact with the brilliant court of Louis XIV and with the leading men and women of that remarkable period. And although she shared the spontaneous *joie de vivre* of that society, its constant flow of highly cultivated pleasures, she nevertheless always retained in word and deed her innate German firmness of character and moral seriousness – qualities that were unmistakably impressed on the strong features of the portrait of this Countess still hanging on the wall. It was this very disposition that enabled her to play in court circles a distinctive role of naive opposition, and in the letters she left behind her there are many instances of her candour and ready wit, displayed equally in matters of religion, literature, politics or anything else. With great originality she would defend her sound principles and views, or criticize the weaknesses of society without giving the least offence. Accordingly her lively interest in such guests as might be met, for instance, at Ninon de Lenclos's house, that true centre of refined intellectual culture, was of such a character as to be wholly compatible with the exalted friendship that bound her to one of the noblest women of the age, the Marquise de

Sévigné. In addition to many whimsical pleas-antries addressed to her by the poet Chapelle and scribbled in his own hand on sheets of paper with a silver floral border, the deeply affectionate letters of the Marquise and her daughter to their good Austrian friend were discovered in an ebony casket by the Count after his grandmother's death.

And it was also from the hands of Madame de Sévigné that one day, on a terrace in the garden during a fête at the Trianon, she had received the flowering orange branch, which she at once casu-ally planted in a pot: here it happily struck root, and she took it back with her to Germany.

Gradually, for some twenty-five years, the little tree grew before her eyes, and later her children and grandchildren tended it with the utmost care. In addition to its personal value, it could stand for them as a living symbol of the subtle intellectual charm of an almost idealized bygone age: an age, to be sure, in which we can today find little that is truly admirable, and which was already pregnant with a disastrous future, a world-shaking calamity already not too far removed in time from the events of this innocent tale.

It was Eugenie who most devotedly loved this heirloom from her excellent ancestress, and that was why her uncle often remarked that one day it would become her special property. It had there-fore been a great sorrow for the young lady when, during her absence in the previous spring, the tree had begun to wilt, its leaves to turn yellow and many of its branches to wither. Since there was absolutely no discernible cause for its deterioration, and no remedy seemed to be effective, the gardener soon gave up hope of its recovery, although in the ordinary course of nature it should easily have lived to twice or three times its age. But the Count, advised by an expert in the neighbourhood, had it secretly treated in a separate enclosure, applying a strange and indeed mysterious recipe of a kind often known to country people; and his hope of one day being able to surprise his beloved niece by giving her back her old friend with its vigour and fertility restored was fulfilled beyond all expectation. Overcoming his own impatience and his anxious concern that the oranges, some of which had by now reached full maturity, might drop off their branches too soon, he had postponed this pleasure for several weeks until the day of the present feast; and we need hardly describe what the good gentleman must have felt on finding that at the very last moment he was to be deprived of this happiness after all by the action of a stranger.

The Lieutenant had found time and opportunity, before sitting down at table, to revise his in any case perhaps rather too solemn poetic contribution to the presentation ceremony and, by altering his closing lines, to fit them reasonably well to the new circumstances. He now drew out his manuscript, rose from his chair, turned to his cousin, and recited his poem, the contents of which may be briefly summarized as follows:

Long ago, on an island in the far west, the famous Tree of the Hesperides had sprung up in the garden of Juno as the Earth Mother's wedding gift to the goddess, and was watched over by the three melodious nymphs. This tree had a descendant who had always desired and hoped to share the same destiny and be presented to a beautiful bride, for recently the gods had also introduced this custom among mortals. After long waiting in vain, it seemed that a maiden had been found to whom the young tree might turn his affection. She showed him favour and spent much time with him. But beside the fountain he had a proud neighbour, the laurel, the tree of the Muses, who aroused his jealousy; for it seemed to be stealing away the heart and mind of the young maiden, gifted as she was in many arts, and turning her away from the love of men. The myrtle tried in vain to console the lover, to teach him patience by her own example; in the end, the long absence of his beloved increased his grief and after he had pined for a time it proved fatal.

In summer the absent beloved returned, and her heart had happily changed. The village, the castle, the garden, all greeted her with the greatest joy. Roses and lilies, their colours glowing more brightly than ever, gazed up at her in rapture and modest humility, and all the bushes and trees waved her a welcome: but for one of them, alas, the noblest of them all, she had come too late. She found its crown withered, her fingers caressed its lifeless trunk and its dry rustling twigs. The tree no longer saw or recognized its protectress. How she wept, how tender a lament streamed from her lips and eyes!

From far off, Apollo hears his daughter's voice. He comes, he approaches her, and looks with pity on her sorrow. At once he touches the tree with his all-healing hands: it trembles inwardly, the dry sap in its bark flows with new strength, already it puts forth young leaves and white blossoms cover it in ambrosial abundance. Yes – for what limits are there to the power of the gods? – beautiful round fruit appears, three times three oranges, the number of the nine Muses, the sisters of the god; they grow and grow, their childlike green turning to an ever deeper gold. Phoebus – for so the poem ended –

> Phoebus counts the fruit, he waters
> At the mouth, and gazes long
> At the precious tree, his daughter's
> Bridal gift. The god of song
>
> Plucks an orange nectar-filled,
> And divides it then and there:
> 'Here's a treat, my lovely child,
> You and I and Love shall share!'

The poet's audience rewarded him with a burst of rapturous applause, willingly overlooking his baroque conclusion which so completely nullified the heartfelt character of the piece as a whole.

Francesca, whose high-spirited native wit had already been stimulated more than once by conversational exchanges with her host or with Mozart, now seemed to recall by chance something she had forgotten, and hastened from the room: she returned with a large brown English engraving, glazed and framed, which had long hung unnoticed in a remote little study.

'So,' she exclaimed, setting up the picture at the end of the table, 'what I've always been told must be true after all: that there's nothing new under the sun! Here is a scene from the Golden Age, and haven't we just relived it today? I certainly hope Apollo will recognize himself in this situation.'

'Splendid!' cried Max triumphantly. 'Why, there he is, the beautiful god, in the very act of stooping pensively over the sacred waters. And not only that – look, don't you see, an old satyr hiding back there in the bushes, spying on him! Upon my word, I believe Apollo's just remembered a long forgotten little Arcadian dance, which Chiron taught him to play on the zither when he was a child.'

'And so it is! What else can it be!' replied Francesca, applauding. She was standing behind Mozart, and turning to him she continued: 'Don't you also notice this branch loaded with fruit, hanging down to just within the god's reach?'

'Of course; it's the olive-tree sacred to him.'

'Not at all! Those are the finest oranges! He's just about to pick one in a fit of distraction!'

'On the contrary!' exclaimed Mozart, 'he's just

about to stop this mischievous mouth with a thousand kisses!' So saying, he caught her by the arm and vowed he would not let her go again until she offered him her lips, which indeed she then did with little demur.

'Please tell us, Max,' said the Countess, 'what is written here under the picture.'

'It's some lines from a famous ode by Horace. The Berlin poet Ramler has just translated it wonderfully for us. It's quite inspired. How magnificent this one passage is:

. . . he who on his shoulder
    Carries a bow that is never idle;

The Delos-born, who dwells in his Lycian woods
And native grove, and on Pataranian shores;
    He who plunges his locks of gold deep
        Into Castalian streams, Apollo.'

'Beautiful! Quite beautiful!' said the Count. 'Just one or two points that need explaining. For instance, ". . . carries a bow that is never idle". I suppose that must simply mean: who has always been a very hardworking fiddler. But by the way, my dear Mozart: you are sowing discord between two tender hearts.'

'I hope not – how so?'

'Eugenie is envious of her friend, and well she may be.'

'Aha! You have noticed my weakness already. But what does the bridegroom say?'

'I will turn a blind eye once or twice.'

'Very well; we shall use our opportunity. But don't be alarmed, Baron; there's no danger, unless this god will lend me his features and his long yellow hair. I wish he would! In exchange he could have Mozart's pigtail and its most handsome ribbon.'

'But Apollo,' laughed Francesca, 'would then have to work out a seemly way of plunging his new French hairstyle into the Castalian stream.'

Amid these and similar pleasantries the general merriment and high spirits continued to increase. The men, as the wine flowed, warmed to the occasion; a number of healths were drunk, and Mozart, as was his habit, began speaking in verse. In this he was backed up by the Lieutenant, and the Count tried his hand as well, occasionally with remarkable success. But such trifles are lost in the retelling, and scarcely bear repetition: for the very thing that made them irresistible at the time and place, the general festive mood, the brilliance and joviality of personal expression in words and looks, is missing.

Among others, a toast in the master's honour was proposed by the old lady, Francesca's aunt, promising him a further long series of immortal works. '*A la bonne heure*, and amen to that!' exclaimed Mozart, heartily clinking glasses with her. Whereupon the Count, with a powerful voice and accurate intonation, began an impromptu song of his own devising:

May the gods inspire his heart
   To delightful works of art –

Max (continuing):

Of which Da Ponte and the clever
Schikaneder know nothing whatever –

Mozart:

Nor, God bless him, does the composer:
He should know, and he's no wiser!

The Count:

As for that Italian fop
Signor Bonbonnière, the wop,
The arch-crook, let's wish he may
Live on to hear them all one day!

Max:

May he live a hundred years, say I –

Mozart:

Or may the devil by that time fly –

All three (con forza):

Off with him and his works to we-know-where,
Our sweet-toothed Monsieur Bonbonnière!

The Count had by now got so much into the
way of singing that this improvised trio soon developed from a repetition of its last four lines into a
so-called finite canon, and Francesca's aunt had

humour or self-assurance enough to join in with her frail soprano voice, adding a variety of suitable embellishments. Mozart promised afterwards that as soon as he had time he would elaborate this little jest into a musically correct composition, dedicated expressly to the present company; and this indeed he did later on after his return to Vienna.

Eugenie in the meantime had long been carefully studying her precious keepsake from the grove of the fierce Tiberius; the company now with one accord demanded to hear the duet sung by the composer and herself, and her uncle was happy at the chance to show off his voice again in the chorus. And so everyone rose from table and hastened into the big drawing-room next door where the piano stood.

Enchanted though everyone was by this exquisite piece, its very theme led them all, by an easy transition, to a high point of merrymaking at which the music as such was no longer of primary importance; and it was our friend himself who first gave the signal for this by jumping up from the piano, approaching Francesca, and as Max willingly reached for his violin, persuading her to dance a slow waltz with him. Their host was quick to extend a similar invitation to Mozart's wife. In a trice the servants, to make more room, had busily shifted all the movable furniture out of the way. By the end of it everyone had had to take their turn, and the old lady was by no means displeased when the gallant Lieutenant led her out to a minuet, indeed it had the effect of entirely rejuvenating her. Finally, as Mozart was dancing the last round with the bride-to-be, he was able to claim in full his promised right to her rosy lips.

Evening had fallen, the sun was about to set, and at last it was pleasant out of doors; the Countess therefore proposed to the ladies that they might like to take the air in the garden. The Count on the other hand invited the gentlemen to the billiard room, for it was well known that Mozart was very fond of the game. The company thus divided into two groups, and we for our part will follow the ladies.

After strolling up and down the main avenue once or twice they climbed a small rounded hill, half surrounded by a high vine-covered trellis, which offered a view of the open country, the village and the highroad. The last rays of the autumn sunlight were glowing red through the vines.

'Would this not be a quiet and pleasant place to sit,' said the Countess, 'if Madame Mozart were willing to tell us something about herself and her husband?'

Constanze was quite willing to do so, and they all sat down very comfortably on chairs which had been drawn up and placed in a circle.

'I will gladly oblige,' she said, 'with something you would have had to hear in any case, as I am planning a little jest in connection with it. I have taken it into my head to make the young Countess, as a happy memento of her betrothal day, a rather special kind of present, which is so far from being an object of luxury or fashion that only a knowledge of its history can make it halfway interesting.'

'Whatever can it be, Eugenie?' said Francesca. 'I think it must be a certain famous man's inkpot, at least.'

'Not a bad guess! You will see the treasure very shortly, it's packed in our trunk. Now I'll tell you my story, which with your permission shall go back a little way.

'The winter before last I was getting more and more worried about Mozart's state of health: he was feverish, and increasingly irritable and frequently depressed. His spirits rose sometimes when he was in company, often higher than was really natural, but at home would mostly be turned in on himself, brooding and sighing and complaining. The doctor recommended a diet and Pyrmont water and country walks. The patient paid little attention to this good advice; such a cure was inconvenient and time-consuming and ran clean contrary to his daily routine. So then the doctor put the fear of God into him, gave him a long lecture on the properties and circulation of human blood and the little round things in it, and on breathing and phlogiston – a whole lot of things you never heard of; and on what nature's intentions really are when we eat and drink and digest, which Mozart had been as innocent about until now as his little five-year-old son. And indeed, this lesson made a certain impression on him. The doctor had scarcely been gone half an hour when I found my husband in his room looking pensively but happily at a walking-stick, which he'd searched for in a cupboard among other old things and luckily found; I'd never have thought he'd even have remembered it. It had belonged once to my father – a fine cane with a big knob made of lapis lazuli. No one had ever seen Mozart with a walking-stick, and I couldn't help laughing.

"'You see,' he cried, 'I'm just about to throw myself wholeheartedly into my cure. I shall drink that water, take some open-air exercise every day, and use this stick to do so. And I've had a few ideas in this connection. It's not for nothing, I thought, that other people, respectable mature men, can't do without a walking-stick. Our neighbour the Commercial Councillor never crosses the street to visit his old crony without taking his stick with him. Professional men and officials, lawyers, merchants and their clients – when they take a walk out of town with their families on a Sunday, every one of them's accompanied by his well-used, honest cane. In particular I've often noticed those worthy citizens standing around in groups in front of St Stephen's Cathedral, having a bit of a gossip just before the sermon and the Mass begin: you can see it very well there, you can see every one of their quiet virtues, their industry and orderliness and equable temper and contentment, leaning, half sitting, well propped up as it were on their trusty sticks. In short, there must be some-thing of a blessing and a special consolation in this age-old habit, rather tasteless though I must say it is. Believe it or not, I can hardly wait for my first constitutional outing with this good companion, my first walk over the bridge to the Rennweg! We've made each other's acquaintance now, and I hope we shall be partners for life."

'That partnership didn't last long. From their third outing together he returned without his good companion. Another was purchased, which kept faith for a little while longer, and it was certainly to this fancy for walking-sticks that I gave much of the credit for the fact that for three weeks Mozart persevered tolerably well in following his doctor's advice. And the consequent improvements were soon to be seen: we'd almost never known him so fresh, so cheerful and in such an equable temper. But alas, before long he went back to his old excesses, and I was in constant trouble with him about this. And then it happened that one evening, exhausted by the work of a busy day and when it was already late, he went out to a musical soirée to please a few inquisitive visitors – only for an hour, he vowed and swore to me. But it's on those very occasions, once he's settled at the piano and in the mood, that people most misuse his good nature; for there he sits, like the little man in a Montgolfier, hovering six miles above the earth where he can no longer hear bells chime. I sent our servant twice to him in the middle of the night, but it was no use, he couldn't get to his master. So at last my husband came home at three in the morning. I made up my mind that I would be seriously cross with him for the rest of the day.'

Madame Mozart here passed over certain details in silence. The fact is that another of the guests at that soirée would in all likelihood have been a young singer, a certain Signora Malerbi, to whom Constanze had good reason to object. This lady from Rome had been appointed at the Opera thanks to Mozart's intervention, and there was no doubt that it was largely by her coquettish wiles that she had won the master's favour. Some even said that she had had him seriously in tow for several months and led him a terrible dance. Whether this was entirely true or much exaggerated, it is certain that she later behaved with great insolence and ingratitude and would even make mocking remarks about her benefactor. It was entirely typical of her that she once described him outright to one of her more fortunate admirers as *un piccolo grifo raso*, a shaven little pig-snout. This witticism, worthy of the arts of Circe, was all the more wounding for containing, it must be admitted, a modicum of truth.

On his way home from that same soirée, at which as it happened the singer had in any case failed to appear, one of his friends, in a convivial moment, indiscreetly let fall to the master her malicious remark. Mozart did not take this in good part, for it was in fact the first clear proof he had

had of the complete heartlessness of his protégée. In sheer indignation he did not at first even notice the chilly reception he was given at his wife's bedside. Without pausing to think, he poured out his story of the insult, and from this candour it may no doubt be concluded that there was no great guilt on his conscience. She even felt rather sorry for him. But she had made up her mind, he was not to get away with it so easily. When he woke from a heavy sleep just after midday, he found that neither his little wife nor the two boys were at home, but that the table had been neatly laid for him with a solitary lunch.

Few things ever made Mozart so unhappy as when all was not going smoothly and well between him and his better half. And if only he had known what further burden of anxiety she had carried about with her for the last few days! It was indeed serious trouble, and as always she had been sparing him the knowledge of it for as long as possible. Their ready cash was all spent, and there was no immediate prospect of any further income. Although he was unaware of this domestic crisis, his heart was nevertheless despondent in a way that seemed in keeping with her state of constriction and helplessness. He had no appetite and no wish to stay indoors. He at once got fully dressed, if only to escape from the stifling atmosphere of the house. He left an open note for her with a few lines written in Italian: 'You have roundly rebuked me and it serves me right. But please, I beg you, forgive me, and be laughing again when I get back. I've a good mind to become a Carthusian and a Trappist; I promise you, I could cry my eyes out.' And off he went, taking his hat but leaving his stick behind; it had served its turn.

Having taken over our narrative from Constanze up to this point, let us continue it in the same fashion a little further.

Leaving his lodging by the market and turning right towards the Civic Arsenal, our good friend sauntered – it was a warm, rather overcast summer afternoon – in a pensive and leisurely manner across the so-called Hof or Court Square and then past the parish church of Our Lady in the direction of the Schottentor; here he walked up the Moelkerbastei on his left on to the fortifications and thereby avoided meeting several acquaintances who were just entering the city. Although unmolested by a sentry who paced silently to and fro between the cannon, he paused here only briefly to enjoy the fine view across the green expanse of the glacis, beyond the suburbs to the Kahlenberg and southwards towards the Styrian Alps. The tranquil beauty of the natural scene was out of keeping with his inner state. With a sigh he continued his walk, along the esplanade and then through the Alser district, without any particular destination in mind.

At the end of the Währinger Gasse there was an inn with a skittle-alley; its landlord, a ropemaker, was well known to passing neighbours and countrymen for the fine quality both of his wares and of his wine.

The sound of bowling could be heard, but with a dozen guests at most little else was going on. A scarcely conscious impulse to forget himself for a while among simple and natural people moved the composer to join this company. At one of the tables, which were partly shaded by trees, he sat down beside an inspector of wells from Vienna and two other worthy citizens, ordered a glass and joined with a will in their very commonplace conversation, from time to time rising to walk about or watch the game in the skittle-alley.

Close to the latter, at one side of the house, was the ropemaker's open shop, a small room stuffed full of his wares, for in addition to the immediate products of his own craft there were a number of other things standing around or hanging up for sale: all kinds of wooden utensils for the kitchen or the cellar, farm implements, blubber and axle grease, and an assortment of seeds such as dill and caraway. A young girl, whose business it was to serve the guests as a waitress and also to look after the shop, was just dealing with a peasant who, holding his little son by the hand, had come in to buy a few things: a fruit measure, a brush, a whip. He would select one among many similar articles, examine it, put it down, pick up a second and a third and then revert irresolutely to the first, evidently unable to make up his mind. The girl left him several times to wait on customers, then came back, tirelessly attempting to ease his choice and make it acceptable to him, though without too much persuasive talk.

Mozart, sitting on a bench by the skittle-alley, watched and listened to all this with the greatest pleasure. And much as he appreciated the kind and sensible behaviour of the girl and the calm seriousness in her attractive features, it was the peasant who chiefly aroused his interest, and who now, after he had gone away finally satisfied, continued to give him food for thought. He had found himself fully identifying with the man, feeling how seriously he had taken his small piece of business, how anxiously and conscientiously he had considered and reconsidered the prices, although they differed by only a few pence. He thought of the man coming home to his wife, telling her what a good bargain he has made, and the children all watching for his knapsack to be opened in case there was something for them in it too; and his wife hurrying to serve him the light meal and the cool glass of home-brewed apple cider he has saved up all his appetite for till now!

If only one could be so happy, he reflected, so independent of other people, so entirely relying on Nature and her bounty, however hard one might have to work for it! And yet even if my art does impose a different task on me, one after all that I would not exchange for any other in the world: even so, why does this mean that I must live in circumstances that are the very opposite of such an innocent, simple existence? If only I had a small property, a little house at the edge of a village in lovely countryside, what a new lease of life that would be! Busy all morning with my scores, and

66

the rest of the time with my family; planting trees, inspecting my fields, going out with the boys in autumn to shake down the apples and pears; sometimes a trip into town for a performance or whatever it might be, from time to time inviting a friend or two home – how wonderful! Ah well, who knows what may yet happen.

He went up to the shop, spoke kindly to the girl, and began to take a closer look at her wares. Many of them were directly associated with his idyllic daydream, and this gave the clean, pale, polished look and even the smell of the various wooden implements a particular appeal. It suddenly occurred to him to buy a number of the things for his wife, choosing what he thought she would like and find useful. The garden tools were the first to catch his eye. About a year ago Constanze had in fact, at his suggestion, rented a small allotment outside the Kärntner Tor and was growing some vegetables on it; accordingly he now judged that a large new rake, together with a smaller one and a spade, would meet the case. As he then considered further possibilities, it does great credit to his sense of thrift that after that brief reflection, though unwillingly, he resolved not to buy a butter-keg which greatly caught his fancy; though he did decide in favour of a tall wooden vessel designed for some uncertain purpose, with a lid and an attractive handle. It was made from narrow staves of two kinds of wood, alternately light and dark, tapering towards the top and well coated with pitch on the inside. As indispensable kitchen equipment he chose a fine selection of wooden spoons, rolling-pins, chopping-boards, and plates in all sizes, as well as a very simply constructed salt container which could be hung on the wall.

Finally he looked long and hard at a stout stick and its leather-covered handle properly studded with round brass nails. Noticing that this too seemed to tempt her eccentric customer, the young saleswoman remarked with a smile that it was not really quite suitable for a gentleman.

'You are quite right, my dear,' he replied. 'Sticks like this are for butchers' journeymen; away with it, I will not have it. But please deliver to my house today or tomorrow all these other things we have chosen.' So saying, he told her his name and address. He then returned to his table to finish drinking; of his three companions only one, a master tinsmith, was still sitting there.

'Well, it's a lucky day for our waitress,' remarked the man. 'Her cousin allows her a penny or two in the florin for the sales in the shop.'

At this, Mozart was doubly glad of his purchases; but his interest in the girl's welfare was soon to increase still further. For when she approached again, the tinsmith called out to her: 'And how are things with you, Crescence? How's your locksmith? Won't he soon be working his own iron?'

'Oh, goodness me,' she answered as she hurried off, 'I think that iron's still growing back there in the mountain.'

'She's a good girl,' said the tinsmith. 'She kept house for her stepfather for years, and nursed him in his illness, and then when he was dead it came to light that he had spent all her money. Since then she's been in service with her kinsman, does all the work in the shop and in the inn and with the children. She's friendly with a fine young fellow and would like to marry him, the sooner the better; but there are difficulties there.'

'What difficulties? I suppose he has no money either?'

'They've both got savings, but not enough. And now the half share of a house, with a workshop, is coming up for auction soon; it would be easy for the ropemaker to lend them the balance of the purchase price, but of course he doesn't want to lose the girl. He has good friends in the city council and in the guild, so now the young fellow finds himself blocked at every turn.'

'Damnation!' exclaimed Mozart, quite startling the tinsmith, who looked about him to see if anyone was listening. 'And is there no one here who can speak up for what's right and just? No one to put the fear of God into that fellow? The scoundrels! Just wait, you'll get your come-uppance yet!'

The tinsmith, mortally embarrassed, tried ineptly to tone down what he had said, almost retracting it completely; but Mozart would not listen to him. 'Be ashamed of yourself to talk like that!' he said. 'That's how you contemptible wretches always behave if you ever have to stand up and be counted.' And with that he unceremoniously turned his back on the poltroon. But as he passed the waitress, who had her hands full with new guests, he murmured: 'Come early tomorrow; and give my greetings to your sweetheart. I hope things will turn out well for you both.' She was quite taken aback and had neither the time nor the presence of mind to thank him.

He set off first by the way he had come, walking more quickly than usual in the excitement to which the scene had roused him; but on reaching the glacis he took a detour and followed the city walls round in a wide half-circle at a more leisurely pace. Busily pondering the affairs of the unfortunate young couple, he thought in turn of a whole series of his acquaintances and patrons who might be able in one way or another to intervene in the matter. Since, however, it would be necessary to get further particulars from the girl before deciding on any action, he resolved to wait calmly until he heard them; and in the meantime his heart and mind, hastening ahead of his footsteps, were filled with the anticipation of getting home to his wife.

Inwardly he felt quite sure that she would welcome him affectionately and indeed joyfully, that she would kiss and embrace him on the very threshold, and longing quickened his pace as he entered the Kärntner Tor. Near it he heard his name called by the postman, who handed him a small but weighty package, addressed in an honest and meticulous hand which he instantly recognized. He stepped into the nearest shop with the messenger to sign for it; then, back in the street and unable to contain his impatience until he reached his house, he tore open the seals and devoured the letter half walking and half standing.

'I was sitting at my sewing-table,' continued Madame Mozart at this point in her narrative to the ladies, 'when I heard my husband coming up the stairs and asking the servant whether I was at home. His step and his voice seemed to me more sprightly and assured than I expected and than I really liked to hear. He went first to his room and then came straight to me. "Good evening!" he said. Rather abashed, I answered him without looking up. After pacing the room once or twice in silence, he put on a show of yawning, and took the fly-swatter from behind the door, a thing I had never before known him do. Muttering to himself: "All these flies again! Where on earth have they come from!" he began swatting as hard as he could in various places. The noise of this was something he never could stand, and I had never been allowed to do it in his presence. Hmm! I thought, so it's quite all right, is it, if one does it oneself, especially if one's the man! In any case I hadn't noticed any great number of flies. I was really vexed by his strange behaviour. "Six at one stroke!" he cried. "Do you want to look at them?" I didn't answer. Then he put something right down on my sewing-cushion, so that without raising my eyes from my work I couldn't help seeing it. It was nothing less than a little pile of gold, as many ducats as you can pick up with two fingers. And behind my back he went on playing the fool, delivering a swipe here and there and muttering as he did so: "Disgusting, useless, shameless brutes! Obviously the sole purpose of their existence – smack! – is to be swatted dead – slap! – And that's something I may say I'm quite good at. We read in natural history how amazingly these creatures multiply – smack, slap! – well, they get short shrift in my house. *Ah, maledette! disperate!* Here's another score of them! Here, do you want them?" And he came to me and did the same thing as before. Up to this point I had found it hard to keep a straight face, but now I could do so no longer, I burst out laughing, he caught me in his arms, and there the pair of us were, laughing and giggling our hearts out.

"'But where on earth did you get the money?" I asked, as he shook the rest of it out of the purse. "From Prince Esterhazy! Transmitted to me by Haydn! Just look at this letter!" I read:

Eisenstadt, etc.

My dear friend!

His Serene Highness, my most gracious master, has done me the great pleasure of entrusting to my hands these sixty ducats which I am to convey to you. Recently we again

*performed your quartets, and His Highness was
so delighted and gratified by them as I think he
scarcely can have been when he first heard them
three months ago. The Prince remarked to me (I
must give you his exact words): "When Mozart
dedicated this work to you, he thought it was
only you he honoured; but he will not object to
my seeing it as a compliment to myself as well.
Tell him that I think almost as highly of his
genius as you do; and more than that he truly
cannot ask." – To which I add: Amen! Does this
content you?*

*Postscript: A word in your dear wife's ear:
Please make sure that proper thanks are
rendered without delay, preferably in person. We
must make the most of this favourable wind.*

'"Oh, you dear, dear man! You noblest of souls!"
exclaimed Mozart over and over again, and it
would be hard to say which delighted him the
most, the letter or the Prince's approval or the
money. As for me, I must say frankly that it was
the money I was truly glad of at that particular
time. We passed a very festive evening.

'As to the affair in the suburb, I heard nothing
about it that evening or in the next few days, indeed
the whole following week passed, no Crescence
appeared, and my husband, caught up in the whirl
of his own affairs, soon forgot all about the matter.
One Saturday we had company, a musical soirée
with Captain Wesselt, Count Hardegg and others.

During an interval I was called to the door – and lo and behold, there was the whole kettle of fish! I went back in and asked him: "Did you order a whole lot of wooden goods in the Alservorstadt?" "My goodness gracious!" he exclaimed, "has a girl brought them? Ask her to come right in!" And so in she came in the most courteous manner, carrying a rake and a spade and a whole basketful of other things. She apologized for not having come before, saying she had forgotten the name of the street and had not been able to get proper directions until today. Mozart took all the things from her one after another, and with great satisfaction at once handed them to me. I thanked him most warmly and appreciatively for each and every item, though I could not imagine why he had bought the garden tools. He said: "But they're for your allotment by the Wien, of course!" "Oh, good heavens, we gave that up long ago! There was always so much flood damage, and nothing ever grew there anyway. I told you at the time and you had no objection." "What! So the asparagus we ate last spring –" "It was all from the market!" "Now look! If only I'd known that! I only praised it to you to be nice to you, because I felt really sorry for you, gardening away like that; those asparaguses were like skinny little pencils."

'The guests were greatly amused by this comical episode, and I was immediately obliged to distribute some of the unwanted articles to them as souvenirs. Mozart then questioned the girl about

74

her marriage plans, urging her to talk to us quite frankly and assuring her that anything we might do for her and her sweetheart would be done on the quiet, discreetly and without making trouble for anyone. She answered with so much modesty, circumspection and tact as to charm everyone present, and in the end we let her go with very encouraging promises.

'"We must do something to help these young people," said the Captain. "The intrigues of the guild are the least of the problems; I know a man who will soon deal with that. What's needed is a contribution towards the purchase of the house and the furnishing of it and so forth. How would it be if we were to announce a benefit concert in the Trattner Hall, with the entry fee at the discretion of patrons?" This suggestion was warmly supported. One of the gentlemen picked up the salt-cellar and said: "Someone should introduce the concert with an elegant little historical account describing Herr Mozart's shopping expedition and explaining his philanthropic intentions, and this splendid vessel should be placed on the table as a collecting-box, with the pair of rakes crossed right and left behind it as a decoration."

'This was not in fact done, but the concert did take place; the profits were considerable, and various further contributions followed, so that the fortunate pair ended up with a surplus; the other obstacles were also soon overcome. The Dušeks in Prague, who are our closest friends there and with whom we shall be staying, got wind of the story, and Frau Dušek, who is a very charming and kind-hearted woman, asked me if she too might have some part of the collection as a curiosity. So of course I set aside the most suitable of the articles for her, and I have taken the present occasion to bring them with me. But since it has unexpectedly turned out that we were to make the acquaintance of a new and dear musical colleague who is just about to set up her own home, and who I am sure will not despise a humble piece of domestic equipment selected by Mozart himself, I shall divide my present in two, and you may have the choice between a very fine openwork chocolate whisk and the much-aforementioned salt-cellar, which the artist has permitted himself to decorate tastefully with a tulip. I would myself definitely recommend the latter piece: for salt, I believe, is a noble substance, symbolizing domestic bliss and hospitality, both of which we most heartily wish you may enjoy.'

This was the end of Constanze's narrative, and it may be imagined with what delight it was heard by the ladies and with what gratitude the gift was accepted. Back in the house with the men, there was presently further occasion for rejoicing when the wooden objects were displayed and the model of patriarchal simplicity formally presented. Eugenie's uncle promised that it would be accorded no less a place in the silver-cabinet of its new owner and her remotest descendants than that famous salt-cellar by the Florentine master occupied in the Ambras collection.

It was now nearly eight o'clock, and tea was served. But our musical hero soon found himself pressingly reminded of his promise, made that afternoon, to acquaint the company more closely with the 'hell-fire story' which he had with him in his luggage under lock and key, though fortunately not too deeply buried. He consented without hesitation. It did not take long to summarize the plot of the opera, and presently the text stood open and the candles were alight at either side of the keyboard.

How we wish we could here convey to our readers at least a touch of that singular sensation which can strike us with such electrifying and spellbinding force even when one unrelated chord floats from an open window, when our hearing catches it as we pass, aware that it can only come from that unknown source; even a touch of that sweet perturbation which affects us as we sit in a theatre while the orchestra tunes, and wait for the curtain to rise! Is it not so? If, on the threshold of any sublime and tragic work of art, whether it be called *Macbeth* or *Oedipus* or anything else, we feel a hovering tremor of eternal beauty: where could this be more the case, or even as much the case, as in the present situation? Man simultaneously longs and fears to be driven out of his usual self, he feels that he will be touched by the infinite, by something that will seize his heart, contracting it even as it expands it, as it violently embraces his spirit. Add to this the awe inspired by consummate art, the thought that we are being permitted and enabled to enjoy a divine miracle, to assimilate it as something akin to ourselves – and such a thought brings with it a special emotion, indeed a kind of pride, which is perhaps the purest and most joyful feeling of which we are capable.

The fact, however, that the present company were now to make the acquaintance for the first time of a work that has been fully familiar to us since our youth, gave them a standpoint and a relationship to it that were infinitely different from ours. And indeed, apart from the enviable good fortune of having it communicated to them by its author in person, they were far less favourably placed than we are; for a clear and perfect appreciation was not really possible to any of those who heard it, and in more than one respect would not even have been possible if the whole opera could have been given to them in unabbreviated form.

Out of eighteen finished numbers the composer probably performed less than half (in the report on which our narrative is based the only one explicitly mentioned is the last piece in this series, the Sextet). It seems that he rendered most of them very freely, presenting extracts on the piano and singing occasional passages at random or when appropriate. Similarly, all we find on record about his wife is that she sang two arias. Since her voice is supposed to have been powerful as well as charming, we should like to think that these were Donna Anna's first ('Or sai chi l'onore') and one of Zerlina's two.

Strictly speaking, so far as intellect, insight and taste were concerned, Eugenie and her fiancé were the only members of that audience entirely after the maestro's own heart, and the former a great deal more than the latter. They both sat right at the back of the room, the young lady still as a statue and so absorbed in the music that even in the brief intervals during which the others discreetly applauded or involuntarily expressed their inner emotion in admiring murmurs, she was scarcely able to give any adequate response to her fiancé's remarks.

When Mozart had come to a conclusion with the glorious Sextet and conversation gradually revived, he seemed to take particular interest and pleasure in some of the Baron's observations. Discussion had touched on the end of the opera, and on the performance provisionally arranged for the beginning of November, and when someone remarked that certain parts of the Finale still repre-sented an enormous task, the maestro smiled rather mysteriously. But Constanze, leaning over and addressing the Countess though talking loudly enough for her husband to hear, said:

'He still has something up his sleeve, and he's keeping it secret even from me.'

'My darling!' he replied, 'you are talking out of turn in mentioning that now. What if the mood were to take me to start composing again? And in fact I'm already itching to do so.'

'Leporello!' cried the Count, jumping merrily to

his feet and beckoning to a servant. 'Wine! Three bottles of Sillery!'

'Please, no! Enough is enough – my young gentleman still hasn't finished his last glass.'

'Good health to him, then – and let everyone have what he needs!'

'Oh God, now what have I done!' lamented Constanze, glancing at the clock. 'It's almost eleven and tomorrow morning we have to start first thing – whatever shall we do?'

'Dear lady, you just can't do it, you absolutely can't.'

'Sometimes,' began Mozart, 'things can happen in a strange way. What will my dear little wife say when she learns that the very piece of work she is about to hear was born into the world at this very hour of the night, and just before a proposed journey too?'

'Is it possible? When? You must mean three weeks ago, when you were just about to leave for Eisenstadt.'

'Exactly. And this was how it happened. I got home from dinner at Richter's by ten, when you were already fast asleep, and indeed I meant to go to bed early as I had promised, in order to be able to get up and into the carriage in good time next morning. Meanwhile Veit, as usual, had lit the candles on my desk; I mechanically put on my dressing-gown, and it occurred to me to take another look at my last piece of work. But, alas! oh, the confounded, untimely meddlings of women! You had tidied everything away, and packed the score – for I had to take it with me, of course, the Prince wanted to hear the music. And so I searched and grumbled and cursed, all in vain! But as I did so my eyes fell on a sealed envelope: from the Abbé, to judge by the dreadful spiky writing of the address – yes, indeed! He had sent me the rest of his revised text, which I wasn't expecting to see for another month. At once I sat down eagerly to read it, and was enchanted to find how well the strange fellow had understood my intentions. It was all much simpler, more concentrated and yet with more substance. Both the scene in the graveyard, and the Finale up to the death of the hero, had been much improved in every respect. (You excellent poet! I thought, now you have conjured up heaven and hell for me again, and you shall have your reward!) Now it is not normally my custom to write part of a composition in advance, however tempting it may be; this is a bad habit, and one often has to pay dearly for it. But exceptions can be made, and in short, that scene with the equestrian statue of the Commendatore, when the nocturnal prowler's laughter is suddenly interrupted by a ghastly voice from the grave of the murdered man – that scene had already gripped me. I struck one chord, and felt that I had knocked at the right door, that behind it they were all lying ready, the whole legion of terrors that are to be unleashed in the Finale. At first an Adagio came: in D minor, only four bars, then a second phrase with five – I do believe that this will be remarkably effective on the stage, with the most powerful of the wind instruments accompanying the voice. Meanwhile let's make what we can of it here: listen!'

Without further ado he extinguished the candles in the two chandeliers on either side of him, and through the dead silence of the room the fearful chant rang out: *Di rider finirai pria dell' aurora!* As from some remote stellar region, from silver trumps the notes dropped, ice-cold, piercing the marrow and shivering the soul, down through the dark blue night.

'Chi va là?' demands Don Giovanni, *'chi va là?'* And then we hear it again, on a single repeated note as before, commanding the impious youth to leave the dead in peace.

And when the last reverberation of those deep-resounding notes had died away, Mozart continued: 'And now, as you may appreciate, it was impossible for me to stop. Once the ice has broken at even one point on the shore of a lake, we hear the whole surface splitting and cracking, right across to the furthest corner. Involuntarily I took up the same thread at a point further on, when Don Giovanni is sitting at supper, when Donna Elvira has just left and the ghost appears as invited. Listen to this!'

And now followed that whole long, terrifying dialogue which snatches even the soberest of listeners away to the borderline of human under-standing and beyond it: away to where our eyes and ears apprehend the supernatural, and we are helplessly tossed to and fro from one extreme to another within our own hearts.

Estranged already from human utterance, the immortal tongue of the dead man deigns again to speak. Soon after his first dreadful greeting, as the half-transfigured visitant scorns the earthly food they offer him, how strange and uncanny is his voice as it moves with irregular strides up and down the rungs of a ladder woven from air! He demands swift resolve to repentance and penance: the time of grace for the spirit is short, long, long, long is the journey! And now as Don Giovanni in monstrous self-will defies the eternal ordinances, desperately struggling against the growing onslaught of the infernal powers, resisting and writhing and finally perishing, though still sublime in every gesture – whose heart is not moved, who would not be shaken to the innermost core with simultaneous ecstasy and terror? It is with a similar feeling of astonishment that we watch the magnificent spectacle of a violent natural force, the burning of some splendid ship. Involuntarily we feel a kind of sympathy with this blind greatness, and share its agony as it whirls towards its self-destruction.

The composer had finished. For a while no one dared to be the first to break the general silence. Finally, still scarcely able to breathe, the Countess ventured: 'Tell us, please tell us something about how you felt when you put down your pen that night!'

As if waking from a private reverie, he looked at

her with a smile, quickly collected his thoughts and said, half to the lady and half to his wife: 'Well, I suppose my head did feel a bit dizzy. I had sat by the open window writing the whole of that desperate *dibattimento*, down to the chorus of demons at the end, in a single flush of inspiration; I had finished it, and after a brief rest I rose from my chair, meaning to go to your room and chatter with you for a moment until I calmed down. But suddenly an unwelcome thought stopped me where I stood.' (Here he lowered his eyes for a moment or two, and when he continued there was a scarcely perceptible tremor of emotion in his voice.) 'I said to myself: Suppose you were to sicken and die this very night, suppose you had to abandon your score at this point – would you rest at peace in your grave? I stared at the wick of the candle in my hand and at the mounds of wax that had dripped from it. The thought gave me a momentary pang of grief. Then I reflected again: Suppose another man later, sooner or later, perhaps even some sort of Italian, were commissioned to finish the opera? And suppose he found it, with the exception of one passage, all neatly put together from the Introduction to the seventeenth number, all healthy ripe fruit shaken down into the tall grass for him to pick up? And suppose he still felt rather daunted by this central part of the Finale – and were then unexpectedly to find that big stumbling-block more or less already removed: what a laugh he would secretly have then! Perhaps he would be tempted to cheat me of the honour due to me. But I think he'd burn his fingers over that; I'd still have a few good friends who know my handiwork and would honestly make sure I got the credit. So now I left my study, looking up to thank God with all my heart, and thanking your good genius as well, my dear little wife, for holding his hands gently above your brow for so long, making you sleep on and on like a little rat, unable to call out to me even once. But when I finally did get to you and you asked me what time it was, I brazenly swore a couple of hours off your age, for it was in fact nearly four o'clock. So now you understand why you couldn't dig me out of bed at six, and why the coachman had to be sent home and told to come back next day.'

'Of course!' retorted Constanze, 'but my clever husband need not imagine that I was so stupid as to notice nothing! That was certainly no good reason for not saying a word to me about the fine progress you had made!'

'And that wasn't the reason either.'

'I know – you wanted to keep your treasure a secret for the time being.'

'All I can say,' exclaimed their good-humoured host, 'is that I'm delighted we shan't need to hurt the noble feelings of a Viennese coachman if Herr Mozart absolutely refuses to get out of bed tomorrow morning. Unharness the horses again, Hans – it's always a very painful order to give.'

This indirect request by the Count that the Mozarts should prolong their visit was one in which all the rest of those present most heartily joined, and the travellers were now obliged to expound very serious reasons for not doing so; but as a compromise it was gladly agreed that they would not leave too early, and that the company would have the pleasure of taking breakfast together.

The party continued for a while with everyone moving around and talking in groups. Mozart was looking about him, evidently hoping for some further conversation with the young bride; but as she was momentarily absent, he artlessly addressed the question he had intended for her directly to Francesca who was standing near by: 'So what, on the whole, is your opinion of our *Don Giovanni*? Can you prophesy some success for it?'

'I will answer that,' she replied laughingly, 'in the name of my cousin, as well as I can: it is my humble opinion that if *Don Giovanni* does not turn the head of everyone who hears it, then the Lord God will simply shut up his music shop till further notice and announce to mankind –' 'And give mankind,' her uncle corrected her, '– a bagpipes to play with, and harden their hearts till they turn to worshipping idols!'

'God forbid!' laughed Mozart. 'But indeed: in the next sixty or seventy years, long after I am gone, many a false prophet will arise.'

Eugenie reappeared with Max and the Baron, the conversation took a new turn and again became serious and significant, so that before the company dispersed the composer's hopes had been pleasurably encouraged by many flattering and perceptive remarks.

The party did not break up till long after midnight; no one noticed until then how tired they all were.

At ten o'clock on the following morning (a day of equally fine weather) a handsome coach, packed with the luggage of the two Viennese guests, had appeared in the courtyard. The Count was standing by it with Mozart just before the horses were brought out, and asked him how he liked it.

'Very much; it looks extremely comfortable.'

'Well, then, do me the pleasure of keeping it as a souvenir from me.'

'What, are you serious?'

'But most certainly!'

'Holy Sixtus and Calixtus! Constanze!' he called up to the window at which she and the others stood looking out, 'I'm to be given the coach! From now on you'll be travelling in your own coach!'

He embraced his chuckling benefactor, walked round his new property, inspecting it from all sides, opened the door, jumped in and called out: 'I feel as noble and rich as Chevalier Gluck! My, how they'll stare at this in Vienna!' – 'I hope,' said the Countess, 'that on your way back from Prague we shall see your carriage again, with triumphal garlands hanging all over it!'

Not long after this happy scene the much-lauded carriage did in fact set off with the departing pair, and headed for the highway at a brisk trot. The

Count's horses were to take them as far as Wittingau, where post-horses were to be hired.

When our home has been temporarily enlivened by the presence of goodhearted and admirable visitors, and when like a breath of spiritual fresh air they have renewed and quickened our very being, so that we have enjoyed the giving of hospitality as never before, their departure always fills us with a certain *malaise*, at any rate for the rest of the day and if we are again thrown back entirely on our own company.

This at least was not the case with our friends at the castle. To be sure, Francesca's parents and her old aunt now also departed; but Francesca herself and Eugenie's fiancé, and Max of course, stayed on. It is Eugenie that we here chiefly have in mind, for she had been moved more deeply than any of the others by so rare and wonderful an experience, and it might be thought that there was nothing she lacked, nothing to grieve or sadden her. Her pure happiness with the man she truly loved, a happiness which had been given its formal confirmation only today, must surely have eclipsed all other feelings; or rather, the noblest and finest emotions that could touch her heart must surely have mingled and united with that abundant joy. And this no doubt would have been true had she been able, yesterday and today, to live only for the present moment, and now only for its pure retrospective enjoyment. But that evening, as she had listened to Mozart's wife telling her story, she had, despite all her delight in his charm, been secretly touched by a certain anxiety on his behalf. And all the time he was playing, despite all the indescribable beauty of the music and through all its mysterious terror, this apprehension lived on in the depths of her consciousness, till in the end she was startled and shocked to hear him mention his own similar forebodings. The conviction, the utter conviction grew upon her that here was a man rapidly and inexorably burning himself out in his own flame; that he could be only a fleeting phenomenon on this earth, because the overwhelming beauty that poured from him would be more than the earth could really endure.

She had gone to bed on the previous evening with this and many other thoughts touching and stirring her heart, and with the music of *Don Giovanni* haunting her inner ear as a ceaseless throng of manifold sound. It had been almost daybreak when she wearily fell asleep.

But now the three ladies were sitting in the garden with their needlework, the men were keeping them company, and since Mozart was naturally the first and sole topic of conversation, Eugenie made no secret of her apprehensions. None of the others was in the least inclined to share them, although the Baron understood them perfectly. In a happy hour, in a mood of quite unmixed human gratitude, we usually find ourselves rejecting strongly any idea of misfortune or unhappiness that does not immediately concern us at the time. The most telling counter-arguments were laughingly advanced to her, especially by her uncle, and how gladly she drank them all in! They fell little short of truly convincing her that she was taking too gloomy a view.

A few moments later, as she passed through the large room upstairs which had just been cleaned and set in order again and whose green damask curtains, now drawn, admitted only a soft twilight, she paused sorrowfully by the piano. Remembering who had sat there only a few hours ago, she felt certain she must be dreaming. She looked long and pensively at the keys which *he* had been the last to touch, then gently closed the lid and removed the key, jealously resolved that for some time to come no other hand should open it again. As she left, she casually put a few volumes of songs back in their place; an old sheet fell out of one of them, it was a copy of a little Bohemian folk-song, one that Francesca had once often sung, indeed she had no doubt sung it herself. She picked it up and looked at it with emotion. In such a mood as hers the most natural coincidence easily becomes an oracle. But however she understood it, its contents were such that, as she reread these simple verses, hot tears fell from her eyes.

> In the woods, who knows where,
> Stands a green fir-tree;
> A rosebush, who can tell,

Blooms in what garden?
Already they have been chosen –
Oh soul, remember! –
To take root on your grave,
For they must grow there.

Out on the meadow two
Black steeds are grazing,
And homewards to the town
They trot so sprightly.
They will be walking when
They draw your coffin;
Who knows but that may be
Even before they shed
That iron on their hooves
That glints so brightly.